The Diary of Pelly D

GREENWILLOW BOOKS
An Imprint of HarperCollins*Publishers*

The Diary of Pelly D

L. J. ADLINGTON

This book is a work of fiction. References to real people, events, establishments, organizations, or locales are intended only to provide a sense of authenticity, and are used to advance the fictional narrative. All other characters, and all incidents and dialogue, are drawn from the author's imagination and are not to be construed as real.

First published in 2005 in Great Britain
by Hodder Children's Books.
First published in 2005 in the United States
by Greenwillow Books.

 Printed in the United States of America. For information address HarperCollins Children's Books, a division of HarperCollins Publishers, 1350 Avenue of the Americas, New York, NY 10019.
www.harperchildrens.com

The text of this book is set in Adobe Garamond and Futura.
Book design by Chad W. Beckerman

Library of Congress Cataloging-in-Publication Data
Adlington, L. J.
The diary of Pelly D / by L. J. Adlington.
p. cm.
"Greenwillow Books."
Summary: When Toni V, a construction worker on a
futuristic colony, finds the diary of a teenage girl whose life
has been turned upside-down by holocaust-like events,
he begins to question his own beliefs.
ISBN 0-06-076615-8 (trade).
ISBN 0-06-076616-6 (lib. bdg.)
[1. Diaries—Fiction. 2. Science fiction.] I. Title.
PZ7+ [Fic]—dc22 2004052258

First American Edition 10 9 8 7 6 5

Greenwillow Books

In memory of Justin Tobias Berry
1971-2003

When the dust settled, Toni V took his goggles off for a moment and rubbed his eyes. It was only mid-morning and already the heat was fierce. The Demolition Crew in the plaza had stripped down to vests and shorts, with shirts twisted around their waists. They had regular water stops. This wasn't one of them.

The Supervisor's voice rumbled over the site. "Hey! Toni V! Shirking's for losers!"

Embarrassed, Toni V clicked the safety to OFF and hunched his shoulders, ready to drill again. There was an instant dust cloud. That's why he didn't see that he'd hit something until it was too late. He clicked the safety and pulled the drill free, sending a signal to the Supervisor that it was a genuine obstacle.

The Supervisor shrugged, resigned. There was over half a city to rebuild, and they expected him to get results from a new crew made up of kids and tired old-timers. As if he didn't have enough to deal with, bullying stonemasons, Dumpster haulers, and that half-brain bozo who was late again with the water delivery!

Glad the Supervisor was distracted by problems of his own, Toni V crouched low at the edge of the chasm he'd been drilling since sunup. He was way down below the concrete crust and through to the packed earth underneath. The drilling was hard work, even in this part of the plaza, where there had once been grass and trees. A few dead roots still snarled up the hole just below the concrete, but that wasn't what the drill had hit. It was something metal, but not a water pipe or underground cables—printouts showed that nothing like that went under this part of the plaza.

With one gloved hand Toni V swept the muck away. He smiled. It was just a water can after all—the sort of thing you could pick up at any general store. He leaned into the chasm and began clearing away soil and dust. Too bad it wasn't antique or something like that. There was a guy on the last job who'd turned up a whole rubbish pit full of stuff chucked away by the first settlers on the planet, and he'd earned a fortune selling on the black market. Dealers paid silly money for anything old—not something Toni V could understand. Who wanted old when you could have new? Unfortunately, this water can with drill marks down the side was just new junk and completely valueless.

He finally managed to loosen it, and with one hand on the edge of the cleft to steady himself, he pulled the can up. This wasn't so hard—it had a handle on the lid, and it wasn't heavy.

It wasn't empty either. Toni V knew perfectly well what an empty can felt like. He'd lived through the drought—the Big Dry—the one where the kids on every block had to go and buy water from a dealer, then lug it home again. For months they'd all been rationed to one short bath a day, which was horrible—nothing more than a gill-wetting.

He gave the can a little shake. It didn't slosh about, so it couldn't have liquid in it. Too bad—a couple of quarts over his hot back would have been Bliss. Still, the can was pretty battered-looking. Perhaps it had been underground for a while, in which case it could be swarming with parasites. Yep—he checked the lid, and the filter seal had curled up at the edges, showing that it was way past its "sell by" date. Unusable. Best throw it in the Dumpster and get on with the job.

Rubbing one arm over his sweaty face, Toni V loped over the plaza to the collection of pink-and-blue Dumpsters. Three of them were full already—the diggers had scooped up great gobfuls of concrete and soil. The fourth Dumpster was at the far end of the row, near the shade of a flowering cimarron tree. Lush cimarron buds had swelled open at dawn every morning that month, furling closed again at twilight with a cloud of dusky perfume. Toni V stared up at the big yellow petals, suddenly homesick. There had been a cimarron tree right outside his old home in City Three, and he'd sniffed up its scent every summer morning before class. Out of all the big cities, Three had suffered the least damage during the war, and it had already been repaired. This was good, only it meant that Toni V hadn't seen his family in a very long time: Work on the other cities was now stretching into years, not months. Funny how so short a war could have such long-lasting effects.

Up in the cimarron trees, the sawri birds noticed Toni V watching. They stared right back, red beaks opening and closing as they cawed soundlessly. Toni V was almost hypnotized. What did *they* think about the churned-up earth and torn mosaics? Did they remember how it all looked before? He shook his head. The heat must be getting to him. None of the other guys wasted time staring at birds and thinking about other things. Thinking about other things was shirking, and shirking was for losers.

He was just about to lob the water can straight into the Dumpster when curiosity got the better of him. There was definitely something inside the can. Probably not the sort of thing a demolition guy was supposed to be interested in. He glanced around. No one was looking. There was nothing to see anyway. He hadn't done anything wrong. He straightened up and looked back at the Dumpster.

If he threw the can away, he'd never know what was inside.

Why should he care what was inside?

It might be valuable.

His grip tightened on the handle, then loosened. If it was valuable, he'd definitely have to hand it over to the Supervisor, then there'd be all the Rules and Regulations to follow.

The siren blared for water break. The diggers stopped, and dust began to settle on sweaty skin like a cloud of hungry insects. The crew downed tools and headed off to the water vats to pull their ration. It was best to get a move on, or he'd end up at the back of the line with the runts, and the water always tasted brackish when it was dredged from the bottom of the vat.

The line shuffled forward—and there was Toni V, still standing by the Dumpster with the water can in his hand. He was having a bit of a funny thought. The sort of funny thought that jumped up and got you late at night, or deep underwater when the lights were low. It wasn't much of a thought, nothing useful, nothing that would get the work done any better. In fact, it was more of a memory than a thought. He was remembering a little boy with a secret stash of treasure hidden behind a loose wall tile in the bathroom. The treasure had been hoarded over several months. There were shiny candy wrappers, a half-melted bit of motherboard, and a few pencil ends that could just about write.

He shrugged the memory off. He wasn't that little boy anymore, and the children he saw playing in the streets of the cities now were like a different species. Even though he'd only just turned fourteen himself, you grew up quickly in the work gangs. His last birthday had come and gone in a haze of dust and tiredness. Remembering back was pointless and stupid, like being nosy.

Then he realized he was unscrewing the lid anyway.

Inside was a square sort of parcel, bent to fit the curving sides of the can. He pulled it out. There was no harm in giving a quick once-over, was there? The brown paper was thin and crackly, and wrapped around with two or three twists of fine electric cabling. He would have ditched it there and then, if it hadn't been for the faint blue words on the front. He wasn't much of a reader, but he could tell what it said, even though the writing was quite shaky.

He stared at the writing, suddenly uneasy.

The words said: Dig—dig everywhere.

The City Five Demolition Crew had arrived just under a month ago. Most of the guys in Toni V's work gang had been buzzing when they heard about the transfer. Toni V had been looking forward to the change as much as anyone else; he hoped there might even be some nightlife for once. There were plenty of bars for the gangs to drink in, although a lot of the guys preferred the nighttime "bottle and bonfire" parties, held on piles of weed-clogged rubble or in dusty bomb craters. Sometimes they got some girls to go along, usually not.

The gangs were billeted in new prefab apartments around the plaza—all very convenient. They'd had to assemble their own flat-pack bunks and head to Supply for new bedrolls and blankets. It wasn't much and it was hardly home; as often as not, they worked double shifts and spent all their free time asleep. City Five had borne the brunt of the heavy-duty missile attacks, and it needed more than a sweep up and a quick lick of paint to make it look good enough for the General's visit later that year.

A large siren squatted on the entrance to the main apartment building. When it hooted for the end of the shift, the Demo Crew stowed their kits and herded back to the block. They jostled and grouched in a comfortingly familiar way. Near the block door they were met by Hood N's swaggering Salvage Squad. Hood N was a regular golden boy—the guy they all wanted to be. He was tall and wiry, very fit—always crackling with energy. No one complained as he joked his way to the front of the line and swiped his ID at the door. The OK light flashed and passed him through.

Toni V had to wait his turn; there was a long line of young lads pressing behind and an even longer line climbing the stairs in front. It was almost tribal, the way their heavy boots clomped forward and upward. They didn't think about it. They could only be glad that the achingly long day in the sun was over. Toni V was especially relieved to get to the fifth floor and into the apartment he shared with five other guys, all boys about his own age. He'd bagged a top bunk near a window since the air-con was pretty unreliable and it was good to know there'd be some breeze at night. He stripped his shirt off and slung it onto the bunk, first looking around quickly to make sure that no one would notice the bundle hidden inside. As if anyone cared. Of the guys he knew well, Monsumi Q had already headed off to the pool, while Credula N was flat on his back, snoring. Cred N was a fairly new guy, a dropout from junior college who hadn't taken to demolition work too well. Since starting on the plaza, his skin had peeled not once but twice. Now he was raw pink and permanently spaced.

There was no sign of the other two lads who shared the room. They were probably on the first shift for grub, which was exactly where Toni V was headed. In just a moment . . .

Kicking off his boots, Toni V hoisted himself up onto the top bunk, making the whole bed structure shake and creak. Cred N griped a bit, then flopped over onto his stomach. Strangely anxious, Toni V waited until he heard regular, sleep breathing from below. He turned away from the bold list of Rules and Regulations on the far wall. He unwrapped the brown-paper parcel and opened the book inside.

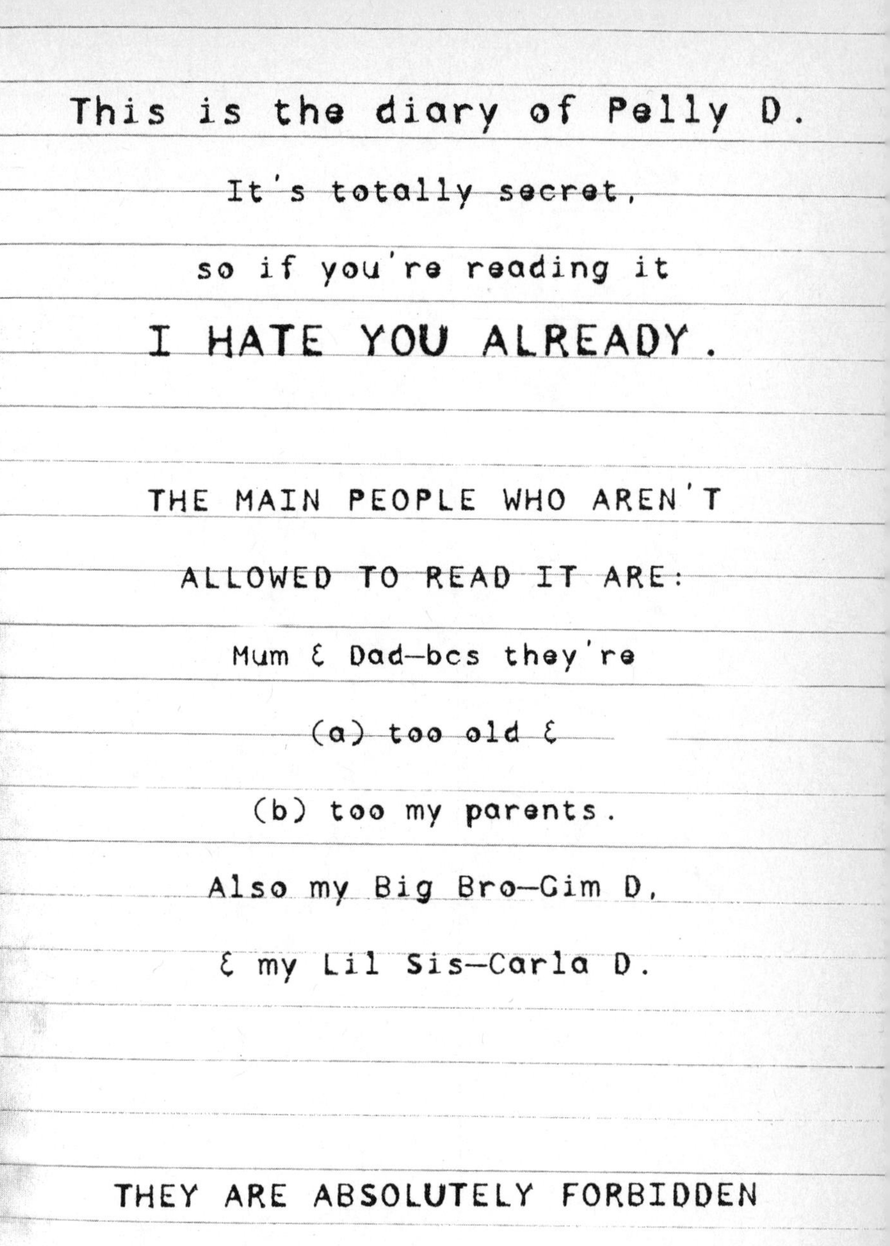
This is the diary of Pelly D.

It's totally secret,

so if you're reading it

I HATE YOU ALREADY.

THE MAIN PEOPLE WHO AREN'T

ALLOWED TO READ IT ARE:

Mum & Dad—bcs they're

(a) too old &

(b) too my parents.

Also my Big Bro—Gim D,

& my Lil Sis—Carla D.

THEY ARE ABSOLUTELY FORBIDDEN

EVEN TO TOUCH THIS NOTEBOOK.

This was not a good start. Forbidden meant *don't.* Toni V closed the diary and lay very still on his bunk, feeling like he'd been caught doing something dodgy on CCTV. Then he decided that the "forbidden" thing didn't count because he obviously didn't know this girl Pelly D. If he was honest with himself, he didn't know many girls, let alone ones who'd bother writing a diary in the first place. He figured there'd be no harm in reading a *bit,* then he could have a laugh about it with his mates . . . and ditch it in the Dumpster later, like he'd meant to all along.

When he turned back to the first page, purple-ink writing leaped out at him once more.

17.5

Spring sunshine on a blue swimming pool. You've got to love it.

Spring Gala at school today. I stood on the winner's podium, up on the school roof with the City spread below. It was like I had my whole life stretched out before me & the whole world at my feet. I turned north first, to get the best sun on my face. North is where the sea is, where the big ships come sailing up the waterway to get to the City. No sign of any on the horizon today. Shame. The City canals were busy tho.

From up on the roof even the streets & buildings looked pretty. I cd just about make out my house, over by the Plaza. Cool. I thought of all the light-years Colonists had traveled to get to this place, of all the centuries of evolution required to breed me. Damn I felt good!

The planet was mine for the taking!

Then Marek T blew the whistle & reminded me that the Gala was actually still happening (I think I could entirely work that out for myself, I mean, shouting to Sassy B over the noise of all the cheering was making me hoarse). Marek T had the nerve to say, would I please step off the winner's podium and get back to my seat?

—Just trying it out for size, I said.

—If you want to win, Pelly D, it'd help if you actually enter a competition, said Teacher's-Pet-With-A-Clipboard.

—Like you'd know anything about winning, I said. (With some justification, I might add. Marek T was only helping out on the pool start line so he wouldn't have to get a gill-wetting himself.)

I stepped off the podium with a lot of grace & a minor readjustment of my swimsuit. That usually does the trick. Yep. Marek T gawped. Let him look. He's not part of my vision of the City. He lives way out by the East Canal, near the wind farms & the recycling center.

& as for winning, I've already bested everyone at the only competition that counts—the School Popularity Stakes. Hey—I got a cheer just for walking along the edge of the pool, without all this thrashing-about-in-the-water-at-top-speed madness.

I brought this diary to school. That's how hard it is to get privacy at home when you've got a creepy older brother & a little sister who thinks paper's for coloring on. God, I hope she doesn't take after Mum & go all arty on me. Why can't she stick to scribble software on the computer?

—What're you writing? Sassy B asks. She always wants to know what I'm doing. I mean, she's my best friend & everything, but I don't know what her status would be if she didn't hang out with me. I'm not being arrogant. That's just the way it is at school. You are who you are—Life's Winners, Life's Losers, & Marek T somewhere after that. I'm Pelly D. It's pretty simple. I RULE!

—It's my autobiography, I told her.

—I thought you already wrote that.

She was so right. I already had—the first fifteen years of my life at least. Then the whole fascinating lot got corrupted by a computer virus. Like the hardy first Colonials, I've switched to paper. I'm so resourceful.

I got this diary from Moma Peg as a reward for . . . for something. I don't know what. Maybe it was just a present & I don't have to earn it, like I do with Dad. Dad says I'll get rewards when I do better in exams (tho I'd like to see him take a nanosecond out of his schedule to say well done the day I hit the jackpot with my grades). Mum's idea of a reward is being signed up for one of her Kinetic Kolor Klasses downtown. Entirely No Thank You! Moma Peg is so much simpler. I think she likes me, & she doesn't like many people. I like her & I don't mind admitting it. She ruffles my hair—the only mortal on the planet with that privilege—& tells me I'm sweet & clever & destined to go far.

Nobody minds that sort of attention.

I don't know where Moma Peg got this diary from. Some of the front pages are torn out. She probably traded it for something, like when I gave her that perfectly decent pair of sun specs & she just swapped them for some piece of antique tat that was only going to go warped in the humidity. Moma Peg trades all sorts of stuff. You'd think she'd've saved up enough to get an apartment by now, but no, she says she's happy sitting out under the cimarron watching the world cross the Plaza.

I sit with her sometimes, but best of all I like it up here, up on the roof of the school, perfectly flattered by the light dancing off the top of the pool. Life is just so-o-o good! I've got the gang (all trying to read this over my shoulder—yes, you, Sassy B, get your nose out of my private affairs!), I've got the guys admiring, & the rest of the world at my feet.

& I've got water on my diary now. Damn. Paper's so useless.

Pick up the pen & write again! (Be still, my trembling

fingers . . .) I've just seen the most offworld guy with the sweetest soft eyes & the best washboard abs in school history. When did HE sign up to Saint-Antel's High, & why wasn't I informed?!

—Who's my new conquest? I asked Sassy B.

One of Sassy B's many good qualities is her ability to suck gossip out of a stone.

—Him? He's in your brother's year—Ant Li. You know, from the Linveki family? Just one of the richest families in City One & big in the Atsumisi Heritage Clan. I heard his parents are here in City Five to manage some rich Atsumisi company, she says.

Like, like & like! (What's not to like?)

Dad deals with a lot of Atsumisi from City One, even with the Heritage Clan. City One is definitely flavor of the month—some big money's being sunk in their new irrigation system. Of course, they do think they're god's gift to the gene pool, but I can relate to that.

Once, about three years ago, Toni V had been part of a gang doing demo on an abandoned factory in City One. He'd been working happily enough, swinging a big sledgehammer into a wall—very satisfying—when all of a sudden he'd trodden in something soft that moved. His foot was stuck in an asci nest. Ascis didn't normally breed in the driest summer months, but the factory was built down near a canal where the ground was soggy from a leaked recycling center, and the little ascis were obviously thriving. Before he'd even had time to move or swear, his right leg had been a swarm of insect life. Ascis weren't deadly by any means. They just made your skin crawl when you had half a hundred running all over you.

And that was *exactly* how it felt reading the last diary entry—as if he had ascis running over the back of his neck; a stomach full of them, even. Toni V checked the name again. Yes, she had definitely written *Linveki*.

That was a bit of a stunner. The Linveki family, as in Linveki Hydro, owned the biggest water company on the planet. Toni V didn't know any of the Linveki family personally of course, not even this boy Ant, who seemed to be such a hit with Pelly D. Toni V had a hazy picture of Ant Li looking a bit like Hood N—all fit and confident and movie-star-like.

As for Pelly D, he couldn't imagine what *she*'d look like.

Rich? Yes.

Stupid? Not sure.

Pretty?

No, probably not pretty, he thought. Probably gorgeous.

Probably the sort of girl who'd be perfect for TV

ads—the ones that showed beautiful people drinking Blue Mountain brand water, their throats tipped back and their lips all wet. Or, she could be in a pool ad, all sleek underwater and smiling . . . and *that* probably wasn't something he ought to be thinking about.

Toni V grinned. For all that she was rich, stupid, pretty, whatever, he couldn't help liking Pelly D. She seemed very much alive and exciting to him. He felt certain that if he ever met her (which, he guessed, was probably never going to happen), he knew that she'd be unforgettable.

Which reminded him that she'd somehow forgotten to retrieve her diary from its peculiar hiding place under the city plaza.

18.5

Not much to write today. Mountains of waffles for dinner, then went to Sassy B's for the usual. Oh, got a new top—it's cute. I saw Marek T gawping from the back of class. As if he's got a chance. No sign of Ant Li. (Swoon & sigh.)

19.5

God I hate that woman! She's not my mother! No way can I be made from HER genes! All she does is go on at me. It's like I can't even get in the door without her pouncing like a mad dog: Did I get to class on time? Did I speak to our beloved Head Teacher, V Gallesi?

No & NO! Getting to class on time wasn't going to happen—not when I had to be at the dock watching the Marie-Cloud berth. She's back from the ocean crossing to Overseas—Santanna Port, I think—then she came up the waterway to City Five. She's such a beaut. I cd live down by the docks—watching the little mail boats skim up & down, all multicolored sails & fresh varnish. The hulking supply ships were clogging up the waterfront—some were in from as far away as City One, but no others from Overseas. Big Bro says the Marie-Cloud's the only ship for him. He's working on a scale model, complete with rigging. I'm not THAT obsessed. As soon as he's done training, Big Bro's signing up. He will, too. Mum'll flip of course. Dad'll do the old I-give-up-on-you-kids routine, then go off to make more money. He's so Atsumisi like that.

Just found out that Big Bro def does have classes with Ant Li. The girls are placing bets on how long before he succumbs to the Pelly D charms. They're so sweet & loyal.

20.5

Mum e-mailed V Gallesi so I got pulled from History class. So-o-o embarrassing. Kasuko C sniggered & everything. Marek T sent a soppy smile—I suppose he thinks he's being supportive. Like I care. Nobody asked me if I wanted to get hauled off to the Head, did they? V Gallesi's got yellow eyes like cimarron. I hate her. No, I despise her. She gave me all the usual stuff—about disappointing Mum & Dad, but most importantly, did I realize I was letting myself down? etc. etc. You're a bright girl, she says, with that whole let's-be-reasonable attitude.

I AM perfectly reasonable! Did she even stop to ask me my motto? . . .

DON'T TRY—DON'T GET.

Simple. Works for me every time. The fact is, I'm not trying for good grades bcs I don't care about getting them. The whole job thing seems like light-years away (well, a couple of years at least) & nobody said anything about needing A-pluses in the meanwhile. I'm Queen Bee in the gang right now—got everyone trying to be like me or be near me. What else do I need? & how much use is schoolwork going to be when I'm off on the high seas in the Marie-Cloud? I haven't told the gang that bit about my future. As far as they're aware, we've all made a pact to take the ferry over to City One to become Successful Something or Others. Dad said I talk so much I'd make a good lawyer. Mum reckons I shd be an artist like her. As if I'm going to spend all day up to my arms in wet clay or paint or whatever she does. NOT my thing!

Moma Peg's all right about it. She said I shd just do as I please. Too bad nobody pays her any attention. That's what you get for being old & fat & sitting under a cimarron tree all day.

—Don't you use sunblock? I said.

—Sweetness, she said, I came out the lab burnt & no skin stuff's going to change that.

It's not true, bcs she once showed me a picture of when she was a girl—about Lil Sis's age—& she's a pretty enough brown like everyone else.

She's not uptight like Mum n Dad. She waddles under the sprinklers when they spray Saint-Antel Plaza every night. I asked her, doesn't she mind when kids make fun of her? But she goes: No little flower, cos I know something they don't. I asked her what & she didn't say. That's so annoying. She'll tell me tomorrow if I take her another bottle of that gorgeous flavored water Dad imports from Overseas, Blue Mountain brand. She likes cherry flavor best. So do I.

23.5

Got Y Bretton for History again. Is he boring or what? If the real teacher's going to be off sick so often why can't they get a good substitute? First class of the day too. I made a totally reasonable explanation of stopping by the Marie-Cloud again & he said "huh" in that feeble way he's got.

"Colonials" again today. Yawn yawn & yawn. I wish everyone wd stop jabbering on about them. Who cares about that old stuff? I think we shd pay more attention to current affairs, & I said so. I don't mind saying what I think. Y Bretton went all serious on me & said we can only work in the present if we understand the past. That's because he's old. He's got a past—a long & achingly dull one. I have a PRESENT & a FUTURE.

Y Bretton wants us all to write a paper about the early Colonial gene pool & how the lab embryos were adapted once the ships had landed & base camps set up. It really winds me up, this whole gene tagging thing. It's such an Atsumisi Heritage Clan obsession. I'm half tempted to believe Marek T (not publicly of course), cos he reckons that the only reason there are the different gene tags is thanks to a big screwup on the Colonial ships when they were on their way here. His wacko theory is that something went minorly haywire with the Cryo (mmm, listen to the boy go technical) so that the test-tube embryos had a nanovariation in their epigenes. When they were grown to fetuses the variation resulted in the Big Three gene families—the Atsumisi, the Galrezi, and the Mazzini. That's his theory. He's been wrong before—like the So Wrong time he tried to ask me out when we were both ten years old, before he got that disgusting upper-lip fluff he likes to think of as puberty.

Still, fetus fiasco or no, the Colonials built a brave new world, & I for one am very proud to live in it. No cars, no violent crimes, & five capitals of Cultural Renaissance on this continent alone. Well, the way City One bang on, you'd think they were the Capital of Just About Everything On The Planet. I suppose it comes from being the first landfall from orbit, it makes them act like the other four Cities were an afterthought. I prefer the theory that each City improved on the last one, tho there's no getting away from the fact that City One is where you go for the Big Time. (If you don't mind being bombarded with propaganda from the Atsumisi

Heritage Clan fanatics; yes, those guys you see on TV all the time going, "Nyah! Nyah! My genes are better than your genes.")

Waste of spacers! Waste of paper, too. Back to . . . back to? Oh yeah, I remember: hurrah for us! Let's face it, we haven't impacted on the host planet's environment (unless you count noise pollution from the Milky Way bar on F-day night!). We haven't accidentally managed to wipe out the planet's indigenous population (there wasn't one). & we haven't any immediate plans to blast everybody into nuclear winter just bcs of some minor diplomatic quibble. Result.

Yep—we should be well pleased with ourselves. Home From Home is a place where everyone lives & works together without fear (read my end-of-term paper on the topic!).

(Brief digression while I imagine self getting Citizenship Award from General Saint-Antel for noble duty to City Five and fellow human beings.)

But you know what? Now that I've started on the

Atsumisi, I turn on the TV & there's the head of the Heritage Clan bleating on at us AGAIN. I can't believe he thinks he's the end product of evolution, this General Insidian guy. I mean, has he looked in a mirror recently? His jowls are so heavy they hang down his face & flap over his collar. He's nothing like our General: I swear Saint-Antel was created from Kevlar, he's so tough & sculptured. He doesn't have time for the whole gene family crap. While the TV companies run graphs showing projected estimates for the three gene families, General Saint-Antel is the voice of reason. Like me.

I say: So the Atsumisi have this epigene, and the Galrezi haven't, and the Mazzini have but it's dormant? WHO CARES? Shdn't someone tell Insidian that he's hogging the Boring Old Fart gene? No one else cares about the whole issue; at least, no one except the Atsumisi from City One, who think they own the continent, plonking their base camp in the best site & telling everyone else to go find their own beauty spot. Well that backfired, didn't it? They've got the most trendy City on the planet . . . & they've had a drought. & now Insidian's activated his I'm-A-Creep gene & he's asking General Saint-Antel to send water from our reservoirs till the City One irrigation system is sorted again. Insidian shd learn to ask nicely: General S-A won't ever let City Five give in to demands from City One.

Marek T says everyone ought to get equal water. What does he know? His family haul their water in by hand—Sassy B told me. I'd rather die than live in an apartment without running water. I mean, how do they fill their pool? Ant Li's got one of those new pools with 3-D hologram reflectors on the bottom. I told Mum & she says we shd get one. They're so cool. Big Bro's seen the Linveki pad already and he says it's offworld. I told him he shd get me an invite. He told me not to get my gills in a twist. I thumped him in the stomach. He wrote "Pelly D's a loser" all over the computer screen-saver & I cdn't work out how to get it off. I hate him.

Toni V rolled over onto his back, suddenly uncomfortable with all this talk of water and pools. He was way overdue for a soak himself. His skin prickled from the heat and plaza dust. He tried to imagine a pool with hologram reflectors; what it would be like to come home from work to wallow, or even to come home from *school* to wallow. He knew that if he was ever rich he'd have a huge pool with the most up-to-date controls for temperature and oxygen and every other gizmo on the market. He'd have a TV in every room, too. No, on second thought he decided he'd have his own movie room, with holders on the chairs for water bottles. He smiled as the fantasy got more elaborate: Who needed chairs? He'd have a big screen in the pool room, with a really sophis sound system so you could lie in the Bliss with just your eyes showing and watch the new releases. If he had a room like that, everyone would want to come around to his place to hang out, even Hood N.

Suddenly Pelly D's pages of . . . nothing much . . . didn't seem so trivial after all. They seemed more like a precious perfect life, where you could easily get pretty much everything you didn't already have. Reading the diary made Toni V forget that he didn't have proper air-con, or holograms or the best Blue Mountain bottled water. Pelly D had them, and for as long as he kept reading he could borrow the luxury. This was how life could be . . . should be!

Pelly D, lucky girl, didn't have to worry about rubble overload and bomb-damaged buildings. If only she wouldn't keep obsessing about the gene thing. He thought it was getting in the way of a good read.

29.5

Double Art & Sport all afternoon. It's too hot for sports. The school pool is off-limits since some wag filled it with industrial foam. There's talk of having a party up there one night, if we can just find a way to hack school security & temporarily disable the caretaker.

When oh when is Waterworld going to open for the new season? They're still revamping the water filters & oxygen tanks. It's going to be awesome—esp if they do all the music events like last year.

Had to make do with sitting by the edge of the North Canal—that place me n Sassy B know about. The grass grows pretty high there & you can watch the boats go by, mostly heading toward the coast. We dangled our legs in the water & talked about everything & nothing. SB agrees with me—no point in sweating the school stuff yet. Got to keep my priorities right. She gets hassle at home too. Her mum's always on at her to Get Ahead. Plenty of time for that. We plan for World Domination by the time we hit twenty. Or at least, dictatorship of City Five. Wdn't that be cool? Somebody's got to do a better job than the City Governors, who are talking of raising the school-leaving age to nineteen. Mum said that wd be good, now that we're all urban & don't need to spend time bringing in the harvest like those smug early Colonists you see in old documentaries, hauling up crops with their bare hands, & big grins on their faces like they're loving every minute of it. Mum just wants me out of the house so she can invite her floaty arty friends over, for her "talking to the universe" meditation classes.

& talking of dictatorship, V Gallesi says she can revoke privileges if I don't make it to school on time. Like

I'm scared! So I'll never be in the first sitting for the school canteen? Big deal. I'll just scoot around the block to the deli, no problem. Missing a few meals won't hurt—got to get in shape for a new swimsuit.

Mum got the quote for the holo-pool. Dad says it's too flashy. He's pretty miserly for a man with a lot of money. He blames the fact that he grew up in a financially challenged family and had to work for everything he ever had in the world. I think he has a pathological fear of losing his stuff . . . at the same time as not being able to enjoy it. He says he never had holograms when he was a kid & he turned out all right. Yeah—that's what HE thinks!

As for Mum, she just spends most of the day up to her eyeballs in clay—literally: in a tank of the stuff. It's called Kinetic Set Art, which, as everyone knows, is just a multisyllable way of saying "mud."

Saw Ant Li by the Plaza's North Fountain, in a real offworld outfit, all open at the neck. I swear he must've had surgery or something to get such a great chin &

that sexy shadow of perma-stubble. He saw me & he smiled.

Moma Peg wasn't there. Sometimes she sleeps near the boatyard. I guess she likes variety. It's not like anyone minds having her in the Plaza. She's been there for eons anyway—when I was a kid we used to think she was a born-again Colonial, with her ratty scratchy skirts & her mad hair. Mum kind of likes Moma Peg—she used to go & play in the Plaza when she was a kid, too. She says Moma Peg's always been like that—sort of singy-songy out-of-her-head-y.

That homeless woman's got more sense than most of the doops at school. If I wasn't so busy planning my conquest of the lovely Linveki lad, I'd miss her.

No. You know what? I miss her anyway. Out on the Plaza with Moma Peg things seem quiet . . . simple.

Toni V smirked. Out on the plaza these days there was nothing quiet, or simple!

Still, it was a nice thought to hold on to. If the next diary entry hadn't looked intriguing he might've left it for a while, relaxed at that pleasant moment.

35.5

I've DIED & gone into orbit!!!! This is it! HE asked me! Not to my face; but he sent a message to Lally B, who told Sassy B, who had to come right over to my place as soon as she knew (yeah—the Net's down again). We're BOTH invited! Can you believe it? Maybe Big Bro did put in a word after all. Well me n Sassy B are heading on over to the Linveki house after school on T-day. Oh yes—to the big Ant Li pad itself. There's some others going too—the usual crowd. No competition. Once Ant Li sees me underwater he'll WANT. Don't know what to wear—the red sequin thing is nice, but maybe he noticed me flaunt it at the movies last E-day. Sassy B's getting something new. I shd. I've seen a darling thing with strappy bits & beading. Irresistible!

36.5

Mum says No Party if I don't get my classes sorted. Guess who's been e-mailing V Gallesi again? I hate them both. I'm GOING to the Linveki place—absolutely guaranteed going to the Linveki place. Ant Li, you don't know what you got coming to you!

38.5

Passed a test just to spite Mum. Also, got my Colonial Gene Program paper back from Y Bretton who says I raise some interesting points. I argued that gene diversity has to be a good thing, else unique individuals like myself wdn't evolve over time. I was only kidding! He seemed to take it all seriously tho & scribbled "on the right track" in the margin. Mum just looks at the grade (B) & says: OK Pelly D, just don't be back late tomorrow night.

She's all mopey again today. I told her not to watch

the news. She says you have to know what's going on in the world. I said: I know what's going on in the world—MY world. She looked at me like my fetus had been swapped in the lab . . . Wdn't that be cool—if she wasn't my mum? Except then I'd have a different one & that wdn't be cool bcs then we might be poor like Marek T. (He's trying to grow a beard—can you believe it, at his age? It looks like some sort of fungus growth on his face! Sassy B n me didn't let up teasing him about it.)

39.5

This is it! The BIG NIGHT! I was in the pool for hours . . . Big Bro & Lil Sis were banging on the door like banshees. Tough luck—that was one long soak. See you later, Pelly D—with all the hot gossip from the Linveki pad . . .

Toni V shut the diary and stuffed it under his pillow. That was quite enough reading for now. It was time to get back into the real world, back to what mattered. He told himself he didn't have the slightest interest in the blistering romance, that he wasn't at all curious about what would happen next. He refused to believe that he could be jealous over a Linveki kid getting lucky with some random rich kid.

"Hey, Mon Q. Is it crowded in the pool?"

Monsumi Q sauntered into the room with a towel slung around his middle. His gills were frilled at the edges with red, oxygen-rich blood, showing he'd been underwater for a while. "Nope—not so bad. Lots of the gang have gone off to the movies—that new Z Homarlo action flick. Y'know, that guy's all biceps—no brains. I reckon we should have a shot at the whole acting thing. Homarlo makes a mint out of it."

"Sure—someday when I can afford to have plastic surgery to make my chin all square, with perma-stubble."

Mon Q laughed, and Toni V felt pleased that he'd made a joke. It was an entirely feeble joke, borrowed from Pelly D, but it was a joke all the same. Quite an achievement for a shy guy.

"I'm not in the mood for movies," he said. "Guess I'll go for a soak myself."

"Later, Toni V."

"Later."

The pool was in the basement, where it was coolest. It was pretty new, but not A1 quality. There were no holograms, for a start. It had been built in a hurry of course, like everything else the crews used. There were the usual stone seats, and long troughs of H_2O that was pumped up from underground then directed into the main wallowing pool. Run-off water collected in a waste pool in one corner, then drained away to be recycled. Working all day in the heat meant that everyone felt grimy when they first got in the water, even though they showered off first.

Toni V undressed and grabbed a towel from the pile—a gray scrappy square of cloth that was none too kind on sun-prickled skin. The moment he touched water he felt the Bliss.

Some guys liked to jump right in. Toni V was all for savoring the moment and letting the Bliss take over his body bit by bit. He swam a few laps, then surfaced, heaving himself onto the pool side—face-to-face with Kiw P. Kiw P was one of the youngest lads in the block and a bit of a runt. It was hard to believe he was actually Atsumisi. He'd started out drilling at the plaza, near Toni V. He hadn't been able to hack the hard graft, so he got a transfer to some minor cleaning detail. Soft stuff. When that job was over, he was put on the Salvage Squad, in the reflected glory of Hood N. Now he was perched on the edge of the pool, smiling nervously.

Toni V's first instinct was to dive back under. Too late. Kiw P said hi. Flushing, Toni V nodded a reply. It was hard to go near the guy without staring. Of course, Kiw P knew what everyone was looking at. There was no way he could hide it: the sides of his neck and face were just ridged masses of red skin where gills had never formed. Whenever he went underwater he had to come back up for air, gasping like a hooked fish.

Toni V took refuge in the water, leaving Kiw P to sit in the shallow end on his own. He swam until the pool was too full of other bodies, then reluctantly climbed out, eyes still averted from the runt.

"Ow!"

"You want to watch that end—there's another crack."

"No kidding!" Toni V nursed his foot where he'd stubbed it on the uneven pool floor. He was shocked to see a blossom of red blood spread out into the water.

Hood N stuck his head around the swinging doors to the changing area. It was like a light coming on in the room.

"Hey—are you coming for waterball at the sports center after dinner?"

Toni V looked up hopefully, but Hoodie was talking to other guys from the Salvage Squad.

Cred N mooched into the pool room, rubbing sleep from his eyes. "Hey, Toni V—d'you fancy going to watch the game? Hood N's squad against the canal crew? Could be close."

"I think I'll bunk up early. I'm kind of tired and all that."

"Sure thing. Later!"

"Later."

Toni V went along to the medic to have his foot sprayed. He hunched over the cracked plastic bench, inspecting the damage with a childish fascination for his own wound. "I cut it on the pool floor," he said.

The medic was a loose-limbed gray man with a big rash spreading over the back of one hand: a rare case of allergic reaction to the wetware ID stamp. He was a godsend to the crews. He could rig up a quick fix on sunburn, headache, heartache, or broken limbs.

"You all right, Toni?" the medic asked.

"Yep."

"Got a headache?"

"No. Why?"

"Nothing. You're frowning."

Embarrassed, Toni V rubbed his forehead. He knew why he had a frown. It was from squinting. It wasn't Pelly D's handwriting—that was A1, he'd give her that much. The problem was his eyesight. He hadn't had to read anything for so long, it hurt to focus. Worse, he was feeling exhausted from thinking so much. His brain felt like his arms and shoulders usually did after a heavy day's drilling—all buzzed up and sore. One minute he enjoyed Pelly D's self-involved drivel; next minute he was tense, worried about the whole situation. There were things she did, things she talked about . . . it was making him fidgety and confused, though he couldn't have said why, exactly.

He shook his head as if he could shake Pelly D right out. No amount of underwater Bliss could change the fact that he was confused as well as curious. So why didn't he just ditch the diary like he'd ditched the empty water can?

Because he still wanted to know.

Why did it say: *Dig—dig everywhere*?

40.5

Pelly D RULES!

Ant Li says I have the sweetest lips of any girl he's ever kissed. Sassy B says he shd know, he's kissed a few. She's just jealous. He's never necked her. See: Don't try—don't get. That's my motto.

It wasn't quite what I expected. I guess he was a bit out of it. The amount of beer they have in that house! The Linvekis run an import/export thing like Dad. It's weird, they've got the big red-&-silver sign on the door—the Atsumisi sign. I never realized they were so into all that Heritage Clan stuff. Ant Li's been going on about the Atsumisi drought in City One. Most of his relatives are back there & he says they're reduced to bathing in bottled water. I thought he was just showing off, but there was a newsflash posted on the Net & it said the same thing. I don't see why Ant's complaining tho, when you think of all the money Linveki Hydro's making from their water imports. Every time I buy a bottle of Blue Mountain brand I'm adding to the Linveki bank account. I read about the old Wars on Earth & someone always profited. Not that this is a War. It's just a drought. It won't come to anything.

Still, given Recent Events in the Smooching Department, I guess the Atsumisi aren't so bad after all. (Mmmmm!) I'll have to call Dad a Galrezi instead—gotta do something to wind him up. It's the latest thing at school, slapping a Galrezi sticker on someone's back & seeing how long it takes before they notice. I don't do it—it's childish & cruel, tho Dad's fair game. V Gallesi too—she's not top of my Fave Things list & when you think about it, Gallesi sounds like Galrezi. But it's not true what Kasuko C says, that Galrezi have personal hygiene issues. That's just one of those stupid rumors, like that joke about the Galrezi who goes into a bar &—.

NO! I will not dignify that joke by repeating it in the pages of this diary . . . even tho I did e-mail a copy to everyone in my address book bcs it was Very Funny. If you like Galrezi jokes. Which I don't. Usually.

More importantly, it made Ant Li laugh when I told him.

No need to write What Else went on above the shimmer of that holographic pool floor—not even for the pages of this diary!! Big Bro might sneak a look.

Hey, Big Bro, if you're reading this—STOP RIGHT NOW.

If I catch him, I'll just tell Mum he's been cutting classes to check out the Marie-Cloud again. OK, so I was with him at the time, but I can take the flak. Big Bro's got to keep on the straight n narrow if he wants to buy a good place on the ship. I told him he shd save his allowance like I do. He stared at me & said he thought I spent it all on stupid clothes. As if. I've got my nest egg. No one else knows about it except me n Moma Peg. She said she's got her own little nest egg. I looked around her "nest" in the cimarron grove & all I cd see were warped plastic crates & empty water cans.

—Not there, sweetness, she said, in here! & she tapped her head—the way other people usually do when they're talking about her & saying she's not all there.

—What've you got in your head?

—More than you'll ever have between your ears, girl, she said, mooching about over boys.

—I am no way mooching! I said.

Anyway, Ant Li's sweet—even if he is Atsumisi. He's been telling me all about the clubs & bars & dealers in City One, in between Other Things . . .

2.6

BLAH BLAH & BLAH.

V Gallesi gave some no-point speech in Assembly

about the importance of neighborliness & multiethnicity. A couple of kids at the back giggled. Weird thing is—she had them sent out. VG is harsh, but that was WAY harsh; I mean, what's her problem? I asked Moma Peg. She did that don't-you-watch-the-news thing. Of course I watch the news. I KNOW what the reporters are saying, but I honestly can't see what all the fuss is about. So the Atsumisi have had another bad year for rain? So they want to build more aqueducts? It's not like we're stopping them. Serves them right for living where they do: the City One planners must've just looked at a map of the planet from orbit, then closed their eyes & plonked a finger down to pick a spot, cos they sure chose a dust-bowl-to-be. Now that's not fair. City One used to have the best water & that's why the Heritage Clan are based there . . . tho now there's one Atsumisi who's very glad he's moved here . . . near ME! That boy can't sit close enough to me in the canteen. I love looking across & seeing him there. (Wonder if anyone's noticed how red my chin is from snogging all that stubble?)

Anyway, I don't mind if the drought goes on a leetle bit longer, cos then Ant Li will have to stay in City Five. Besides, it'll do City One good to be humble & hard-working for a bit. They've bragged about things long enough—how it's the land that never runs dry. Well, it looks like it has. They've had it good for almost two hundred years & they've made their money. Looks like they'll have to live off pride for a while, won't they, & there's plenty of that in City One to go around. They guard their gene pool pretty carefully—the only people who bother. I think it's freaky.

I'm not saying we shdn't help them—I'm all for government aid n that. General Saint-Antel wd never stand by & watch another City suffer, even if General Insidian is the BIGGEST jerk to take office. I can't believe City One voted him in. He'll have to go, if me n the girls are going to hit the Big Time there. I just refuse to give credibility to a City that has General I as its leader. General S-A is way superior—& quite dishy for an old guy. Think I'll do my end-of-term Current Affairs paper on him. Dad cd fix me up an interview, no probs. Hey—the General wd probably be flattered that I, a mere student, wanted to meet him. Wonder what he thinks about gene tagging. Come to think of it—I wonder if he's ever been tested. People usually do it in secret for medical reasons, don't they? He cd've been tested. Whatever he is, he's cool. He's the one who cleared funding for the new marina to be built to service the route to the coast. Can't wait to see it. Dad shd buy a boat, then we cd get out of the City more. Going by public ferry just isn't the same.

Anyway, if I found out about General S-A's gene tag, I cd double up for the History paper as well. As far as all this posturing about City conflict goes, I just don't think General smarmy Insidian has got a leg to stand on when . . .

Oh, stuff it. I'm not going to waste pen & paper on tedious stuff. What I meant to write was that Ant Li e-mailed me the sweetest little note. I've printed it out (to hell with the paper shortage & helping the environment) & I'm going to keep it here in this diary for ever n ever, & one day when we're both old n gray I'll show it to him to remind him how besotted he was. He'll still be besotted when we're old n gray of course, only then it'll be kind of icky so I don't want to think about that either.

Gladly forgetting all Pelly's irreverent ranting about generals, Toni V flipped quickly through the pages of the diary, looking for this cherished note from Ant Li. There wasn't one. Pity.

He'd never really had a chance to date a girl before and wondered how you went about it. According to Pelly D's diary it was pretty hit and miss: you were either the offworld guy or you weren't—you were the loser like the kid Marek T.

Not that it mattered what this Pelly D girl thought anyway. She was more like an alien life-form than the girls Toni V was used to—real girls who knew how to work, who didn't wait for handouts from Mummy and

Daddy. There had been one girl once, a quiet white-haired girl from City Four who'd told him about her pet sawri bird and let him stroke her hair. For seven nights in a row Toni V had lain awake thinking about her, now he could hardly remember her name—Jully something. On the eighth night she'd told him she was going Overseas; she'd been offered a job at the massive Linveki Hydro factory at Santanna Port. She said she'd get paid more, although the work would be hard. Then she'd gone.

He sometimes wondered what had happened to her. That was the thing about people who left: you never knew what happened to them after that. He hoped Jully was getting paid well and that the work wasn't as hard as she'd thought.

There was no way he could imagine Pelly D working. In fact, the mere idea of Pelly with her sleeves rolled up in the rubble was enough to make him smile. He fancied the idea of Pelly D giving the Supervisor a good talking-to, or flirting with the contractors.

Maybe she'd be fun to have around, even if she wouldn't know one end of a drill from the other.

He sighed quietly, so as not to wake the other guys, who were all sprawled coverless in the evening heat. It was getting late. The block doors were long since shut for the night, after Hood N's victoriously rowdy return from waterball.

Maybe it was time to stop this stupid reading. He needed a proper night's sleep as much as anyone. Still, it wasn't dark, not with the giant arcs of the security lamps blazing out over the plaza debris. It wouldn't matter if he read just a bit more. It stopped him thinking about his foot, which was still smarting from the medic's antiseptic cocktail.

He turned to the next entry.

10.6

Intense! I LOVE that guy. The Linveki family has the most awesome apartment. I'm over there practically all the time now. Mostly hanging out with the crowd, but sometimes I get Ant Li all to myself. He's got a gorgeous smile—JUST FOR ME! Big Bro pretends to vomit whenever I talk about it. Lil Sis wants to know if kissing's nice. Mmmmm—you bet—

Frustrated, Toni V stared at the jagged edges of paper that showed the next four pages had been torn out. Just when things were getting hot . . .

Stupid diary. He stuffed it under his pillow one last time and scrunched down in his sleeping bag. Below, Cred N was snoring. Cred N had had a serious girlfriend once—a big-boned, big-hearted girl with nice eyes that crinkled when she laughed. Toni V had seen the photo. That was before Cred N ran out of money and quit junior college for the City Five work gang.

Toni V thought it would be good when the plaza dig was done and they could move on to another job—somewhere with a bit more social life maybe. He hadn't seen any girls he particularly fancied in City Five.

Would he fancy Pelly D if he saw her?

Of course.

Would she ever look twice at him?

Of course not.

Rumpled and frowning, Toni V drifted off to sleep.

He dreamt of cimarron flowers and girls swimming underwater.

The Big Screen was on during breakfast. About time, too—it had been out of order for so long they'd forgotten what TV sounded like. The picture was still fuzzy, but it was entirely better than nothing. Toni V slid into place next to Mon Q and Cred N. Everyone had their eyes glued as they drank down their vitamins. The weather report was no surprise—hot, and getting hotter. The General came on for a good old get-you-psyched-up-for-work sort of speech and then there were cartoons. It almost made up for heading out to the plaza again. When the transmission ended, the screen lit up with the familiar slogan and a prerecorded voice chanted: "Back to Work, Back to Normal." The crews repeated it faithfully and stood up ready to file out. Hood N's salvage team went off first, with the runt Kiw P at the back, his cap pulled down low.

Obviously Toni V kept expecting to drill into another water can. Stupid really, and kind of funny, too. The brown paper had said *Dig—dig everywhere*—and wasn't that what they were doing? The north fountain was long gone, and guys were just starting work on the west cascade, swinging great masonry hammers high overhead, then bringing them down—*wumph!*—onto the stonework. Over half the plaza was broken up, waiting to be cleared.

He wondered if anyone else had found things. It wasn't usual for Demo Crews to scavenge—they were normally just clearing up after the Salvage Squad had picked over the rubble. No, it wasn't usual for the Demo Crew to find things.

It wasn't usual for people to bury things in a public

plaza, either, but they obviously had. Did that mean that there could be other guys on the block curled up on their bunks furtively reading like him? No way of knowing. There were usually six to eight guys per room and maybe two hundred rooms per block . . . and how many blocks in the city had been requisitioned for workers? That made a lot of people digging. Of course, reading stuff like the diary was against the Rules and Regulations. It was the sort of document he ought to report. Maybe he could hand it in to the Supervisor, let him deal with it, or just chuck it in the skip, or lob it in the canal. He was an excavator, not a . . . not a person who was interested in rubbish found on a building site.

Thinking about building was much more relaxing than thinking about diaries—it was something he knew.

One strip south of the plaza was being redeveloped into deluxe new apartments: lovely living space for everyone—the General's promise. The General said they were building a brave new world over the mistakes of the past. The General said they should all thrive on the spirit of the times by joining the O-HA, the Overseas Humanitarian Agency. Toni V didn't know much about the O-HA, though he'd seen their smart silver badges on all sorts of people. The O-HA had started out as an agency that shipped A1-quality water supplies from Santanna Port, Overseas, across the ocean to any of the cities that needed it. Now it was a pro-peace megacharity doing general good things on both continents. If you joined the O-HA you got a little tattoo next to your hand ID—a picture of a silver mountain—and you could get a special O-HA e-mail account and newsletter, and invitations to the big O-HA rallies. Lots of people joined the O-HA. Lots of girls joined. It didn't cost that much. . . .

Toni V put this thought aside for later. The Supervisor always said you should concentrate on the job at hand, otherwise there'd be mistakes. Razing five-story apartment blocks or tearing up paving slabs might look like gung ho anarchy but it took concentration to keep it safe. No one had told them why the old blocks were being flattened, of course. They were probably just weakened by missiles from the war, or resistance sabotage. It was all the same to the Demo Crews, or it should be. Toni V worried that he might be too curious, wanting to know stuff like that. In a few years' time he would graduate to adulthood. He'd become known as T Vedeki; he'd be Somebody. He could get on the waiting list for his own place, if he saved enough money. In the meanwhile perhaps he'd better keep his head down and follow the routine like everyone else.

Just as the TV had predicted, it was hotter than the day before. The Supervisor had set his work table up under the cimarron trees in the grove and was energetically banging away at his laptop. It didn't like the heat any more than the workers did. Toni V thought the supe was mad to bring the computer out: he wouldn't trust anything to stay clean in all the dust. That set him thinking, as the powerful monotony of the drill sent giddy vibrations up his arms and into his shoulders.

How would he keep something dust-free and protected out in the plaza? Would he wrap it in brown paper and put it in a water can?

He scowled, reminding himself that he wasn't a kid collecting junk anymore. What would he put in a water can anyway? He had nothing to write about and nothing to hide. He followed the General; he followed the Rules and Regulations. He was good at his job, good at demolishing things. He was tearing up the plaza at pace.

13.6

My life is a (well-dressed) tragedy.

I'm NEVER going to write that boy's name again. Or say it. Or think it. I can't BELIEVE . . . !

Oh what's the point? Sassy B says that any boy who gets stroppy bcs a girl won't do THAT straight-off isn't worth knowing anyway. Easy for her to say. She wasn't saying no to the sexiest guy on the planet, THAT B*****D, was she? It's not like I didn't want to—of course I did. Only it didn't have to be at that very moment, did it? I'd promised Big Bro I'd meet him at the Plaza, north corner near Hanger Lane. He'd gone to the trouble of getting a couple of onboard passes for the Marie-Cloud after all. The Nameless B*****D did that smile thing & said Gim D cd wait whereas HE was all thirsty & burning up.

So we were in the holo-pool?

So I fancied him so much it makes my head dizzy?!

That doesn't mean he shd get all . . . oh, never mind. La la la, I don't care.

I don't care what he said, either. Typical Atsumisi. They'll call anyone Galrezi when they're mad at them. It's so common. The whole Linveki family is common, with their snobby obsessions about heritage. They shd all be shipped back to Earth & abandoned there along with all the Atsumisi Heritage Clan, General Insidian included. Since they like squabbling so much they'll feel right at home on the planet that perfected the art & science of Warfare. I mean, GROW UP, Atsumisi! GROW UP, Ant Linveki!

He was boasting about the red-&-silver Atsumisi ID on his hand, a sign that he's into the Heritage Clan stuff. According to me (Queen of what's cool & what's just crap), this hand ID business is Trying Too Hard to be cool. Tattoos are one thing, but no way am I having that wetware on MY hand, messing my skin. No one's going to take any notice of the new City One law anyway, that says everyone shd be tested for gene ancestry. Mum says they'll never enforce it & it's not constitutional & who cares whether they're Galrezi, Atsumisi, or Mazzini? Yeah, Mazzini: piggies in the middle. Mazzinis are like Atsumisi poor relations: they've got the epigene thing but it's not active.

Not active doing WHAT?!

I want to know! Straight answers would be nice, all you scientist-types out there. I went on the Heritage Clan Web site & they just gloss over the whole issue. I mean, the genes or epigenes—whatever—don't have any obvious effects, do they? A snooty Atsumisi can be as hideously ugly as the next human—white hair, brown hair, crinkly hair, waved: they cd look like anyone. & there's no conclusive evidence that the A's are faster, smarter, better in the water than anyone else. So they have a longer life expectancy? (See how I regurgitate stuff from Current Affairs class?!) The Mazzini are supposed to have better spatial awareness & the Galrezi, well, there's a myth that they're artistic & inspirational.

It's all a big black hole of stupidity. Aren't there more important things to worry about? (Like, getting my life back to normal.) Atsumisi, Galrezi, Mazzini—the names all blur into a muddle unless you stop to think about it. & why shd I stop to think about it? I've got BETTER THINGS TO DO.

People look back to the past too much. The Atsumisi are always blatting on about being pure to the Colony ideals. Well, they weren't actually on the spaceships when they arrived, were they, so how do they know what the first Colonists thought? I mean, everyone came out of pretty much the same test tubes didn't they? Oh, no, I forget, the Linveki lot probably had gold-plated ones encrusted with diamonds bcs nothing less wd do for them. Snobs. I hate them.

14.6

Still not speaking to the B*****D. He can come crawling all he likes. I told Moma Peg what he said. She laughed. I said: Isn't that just like an Atsumisi? & she says: What do you know about Atsumisi? I cd be one, for all you know!

Yeah—& maybe I had a fancy test tube too!

I asked Mum & she went on & on about multiethnicity & not worrying about whether you're A or M or G or whatever. She said: you're Pelly D—that's D for Damson family, not anything else.

It was funny, hearing her say the grown-up name out loud. I guess one day I'll be an adult & be P Damson & all smart & rich & everything. Wonder what I'll be like ten years from now? Space-age lawyer in City One, or, better still, Captain of the Marie-Cloud, I bet, with tons of gorgeous men after me. I'll read my diary again & think, yes, the seeds of genius were there, even as a girl. & I'll send copies of all my Awards to V Gallesi, who'll be old & retired by then,

& she'll wither up & die to think that she ever doubted me or got all "disappointed."

15.6

The B*****D came to our house again. Dad let him in without even asking me. He does business with R Linveki, Ant Li's dad. He was all over Ant Li—bugger, I said his name now, twice. Well, anyway, Dad was creeping, all fawning & showing off. We watched the news together, lounging in the pool in a row. I hope Ant Li noticed that our new holo-pool is way more offworld than his. Mum ordered it from Overseas. I'll say this for the other continent, they may have the foulest weather system on the planet but they make nice pools. (I didn't know, but when it's not raining over there, it's snowing. Yes, snowing, like you see in the documentaries. If that's the New Frontier, I don't see why anyone wd want to go there—unless it's for the pleasure of a sail on the Marie-Cloud, of course). The new pool took a whole three weeks to arrive, which is forever when you're waiting, but that's how long the ocean crossing is. Big Bro headed off to the docks to watch the freighter come in. He's always sneaking off like that—he cadges lifts to the seaport on one of the canal boats too sometimes. Reports of rain & snow haven't put him off the idea of going Overseas & "finding his fortune" in the New Frontier. (Never stops to think about practicalities, that boy, like, will there be anything to do when he gets there apart from climb mountains & get cold? Or, have they even built any shops yet?)

One good thing: Big Bro says people aren't so freaked out about the gene thing Overseas. The Atsumisi Heritage Clan haven't worked their "magic" over there so much. Overseas, they've got this thing called the O-HA, some humanitarian thing that sends stuff to us—water mainly. O-HA are totally pro-peace. They totally get my vote then: Hello O-HA!! Fancy a trip over here to sort out civilization? Starting in City Five if you please!

But no way am I going to live on the other continent. I'll stick right here at home, thank you very much. Traveling for three days to get to one of the other Cities is one thing; sailing for three weeks to cross the ocean, well, it'll take a lot more than the lovely O-HA lot to tempt me. Big Bro doesn't see it that way. He's got the Itch. I don't understand it. I have ambitions, yes, & World Domination is almost within my grasp, but why would I want to move & change this wonderful life? OK, OK, there are a couple of minor adjustments I'd make to my life (like disposing of parents, head teachers, & the B*****D) but apart from that, I got it good!

& I got a holo-pool!

It cost a packet of course. Never mind: Overseas are mad keen to do business with us, even with the Atsumisi Corporations in City One—where all the money is. So, maybe our pool costs a packet but Dad's making an even bigger packet from importing water—my fave cherry-flavored Blue Mountain brand. Blue Mountain sponsors the O-HA. Dad says the O-HA is funding a lot of the new irrigation work the Atsumisi are doing.

—So why are the Atsumisi still whining about water if the O-HA are sending so much? I asked.

The B*****D got all stroppy (as if anyone asked him to talk) saying that the A were going as fast as they cd, building the new aqueducts & things, only they'd been so conscientious about their birth quotas (unlike every other City, he meant) that they just don't have the workers. Then he made some snide remark right up close to my ear, about how he'd like to practice getting the Atsumisi birth quota up.

Ooh, ooh, swoon & sigh—like THAT line'll really make me swim the deep end with him.

—Lots of workers are going from the other Cities, I said coldly.

—Not enough, he said.

Yeah, I thought, some people don't know when enough is enough. I let him try & kiss me at the door.

TRY being the operative word. I'll get Big Bro to reprogram the swipe on the front door if Dad doesn't see reason about keeping the B*****D out.

E-mailed Sassy B & gave her the lowdown.

18.6

Sassy B off-line. She told me in class that her account has been blocked. All her family accounts are blocked. No one else in their building has that problem. She sort of tossed her hair & said it was nothing, then she went all pink & wdn't talk about it.

Weird.

19.6

Sassy B called at our house. Big changes. It's scary. I can't BELIEVE this is happening. What's WRONG with our government? Why doesn't General Saint-Antel do anything? I wdn't stand for it! I've started an e-mail letter campaign about it already. Basically, Sassy B's mum has got to go to City One to work on one of the irrigation projects—something about the big recycling plants they need to get City One water levels back to normal. Her mum's an A1 engineer & they need her to go. They're going to pay for relocation, which is good, but the whole family has to go, which is BAD. I said: Well why can't she just go & do the job & come back? Sassy B says it's all the planning & computer simulation work—what her mum's good at. They can't get on-line again till she agrees. That's neighborliness for you. I hate our government.

29.6

They went today. They went the coast route, cos the inland intercity ferries are clogged with freight right now, so Sassy B got to go on the Marie-Cloud before me—& she doesn't like sailing half as much as I do. It was tugged out of the City docks and along the waterway to the coast. They got a first-class cabin, like one of the ones me n Big Bro saw last time we had a tour of the M-Cloud. There's a perpetual motion water shower, two public pools & A1 TV interface with every berth—the only way to travel! It's been a really calm day so they had to motor out, then wait for the winds when they hit the wide water at Orelia Sound.

I was forbidden to skip off school for a few days & go with her as far as the coast. Once she's settled, I'll visit—I'll be off to see the bright lights & big city & all that! I said I'd e-mail her straight off—she said she'd let me know as soon as she had a new address. Yikes—only a few days & everything's changed. She gave me her silver charm bracelet & cried. There was no need to cry. With the sort of money the Atsumisi'll be paying her mum to go, she cd afford to buy herself a whole silver swimming pool now. Actually, I was pretty sad watching her go. That beautiful ship—all the way to City One. Things are great there, apart from the drought right now (and the Heritage Clan bozo-brains). When I'm grown up I'll go there at warp speed, just try & stop me.

32.6

Off classes today, sick. Mum turned the pool up warm & left me to soak with the TV interface. Nothing showing but stuff about the A's, & all the people going over to help. No sign of Sassy B & co in the footage—I was looking out for her shock of red hair & her funny white face. All the other emigrating workers looked tired & washed out. No wonder the new irrigation projects aren't going so quickly.

A couple more kids from our year are leaving for City One. Unfair! They'll miss the big test on early Colonial science—yawnarama. Who cares how they propagated the first crops or set up synthetic factories?

—But Pelly D! says Y Bretton. Don't you want to know how the Colonists made Home planet the way it is now?

—Do I look like I want to know? I said. (I knew I shd've skipped this class.)

—Home From Home is a miracle planet, he said, a place where everyone lives & works together without fear.

—What about the Galrezi? Marek T pipes up from the back where he sits—on his own I might add. (Big laugh at the G word. Then I remembered that the B*****D had used it on me when I wdn't put out.)

—What about them? Y Bretton asked.

Any number of creeps were just dying to spout off everything they'd seen on TV. Talk about regurgitation. All the stuff about the G's not having the epigene that the A's & the M's have.

—& what's so important about the gene that the G's don't have? goes teacher.

Silence.

—Nothing! says Pelly D the fearless.

& once again I am right.

—Nothing, says teacher. It has no effect on physical appearance, mental ability, or sociability. It's a chromosome technicality, that's all.

—How do you know, are you one? some kid asked.

Then I swear, Y Bretton went bright purple, gill tips n all. He just stood there for ages, it was achingly bad.

Big laugh again—but quiet when showed us his hand. I wd've noticed sooner if I didn't already know that teachers have NO fashion sense & so are not worth looking at closely. Once you've seen it there's no missing it tho—a big blue-&-silver stamp on the back of his hand: the same kind of microcellular technology that the Linveki family had used for their IDs. Y Bretton was an M—a Mazzini—loud & clear. First time I've seen one of the gene stamps on anyone apart from Atsumisi. YB says everyone will get one soon. There's no way I'm having MY colors coordinated by the government. I hate blue, for starters—doesn't go with my bonny brown eyes! I'm not having red either, like Ant Li. & as for green, that wd mean being Galrezi, & let's face it, I cd never be so unpopular.

Toni V scratched at the stamp on his own hand. The color had faded a bit, but the imprint was still there—and the information it encoded was still readable by anyone with a scanner.

It was E-day—the end of the working week.

"Hey, Toni V! You sick or something?"

He sighed. This was getting ridiculous. Every time he grabbed a moment to read on, someone interrupted him. This time it was Monsumi Q, bursting into the room with plans for a great night out. Toni V let him babble on for a while, screening out the details of girls to ogle, drinks to down, and furniture to trash.

Mon Q ended with, "Pretty supreme, huh?"

"Offworld," said Toni V, forgetting all half-baked ideas about confiding in Mon Q. He would've liked to talk to someone about the diary, to share some of his confusion and concerns—even his pleasure—in reading it. It was getting harder and harder to snap out of reading and into real life. He was becoming too absorbed in Pelly D's world. She wrote pages and pages of . . . of nothing really, all about her clothes, her moods, her mum, her life—anything. One page she'd be all buzzing with happiness—next she'd be writing a massive essay on why her parents should get a one-way ticket into orbit.

Reading the diary—about the only thing he'd ever read apart from kid's comics, and the Rules and Regs, of course—reading the diary was a bit like TV. It took him away from the parched building site outside and into another world. He read about how she got chocolate muffins on the way home from class; how she went down to the docks and just stayed for hours drinking Blue Mountain and watching the little boats tool up and down the waterway heading coastward; how she staged a walkout to protest about the dissection of sawri birds in science class. In some ways it was better than TV—there were none of the usual *Back to Work, Back to Normal* slogans.

Unlike TV, he couldn't just walk away when transmission ended. There was always one more page to turn, one more entry to read.

So he kept on reading. . . .

Next in the room was Cred N, all togged up in his best shirt, rubbing his peeling scalp.

"Hey, Toni V! It's the big E-day—time to get on the evening fun squad. Quit shirking . . ."

"Shirking's for losers!" chorused the crowd of guys out in the corridor.

Toni V smoothed his pillow flat, the diary underneath. He swung his long legs off the bunk.

"Relax, I'm ready now. Which bar are we headed to first?"

The gang outside grinned and whooped. "Supernova—two blocks away."

"Okay."

There was no time for a swim, so he settled for a clean shirt that would do well enough for group intoxication.

By the time they'd made it to Supernova, Toni V was feeling pretty good. He fought for a seat near the bar. Supernova was a seedy enough place, with prewar decor and cringingly retro music. It was also cheap and noisy—the perfect place for crews to wind down. Cred N made it through the crowd and they sat in silence together—splashing out a week's allowance on Blue Mountain water and black-market beer.

A space cleared at the far end of the bar. Hood N was having a friendly arm wrestle with one of the chunky girls from the neighborhood sanitation squad. She didn't look a bit like Pelly D—or how Toni V imagined Pelly would look.

The lights fizzed in a power surge, then went dead.

Somewhere in a back room the circuit tripped and switched to backup. The bar crowd cheered, Hood N the loudest of all. He was really downing the black-market stuff. His eyes had a slightly manic look about them and he was just exploding with energy. The wrestling spread to other guys in the bar. Next time Toni V looked over, Hood N had Kiw P's head in an arm lock, ruffling the kid's yellow curls with his other hand. Everyone laughed as the little runt struggled to get free. After a while Hood N lost interest and offered Kiw P a drink instead—no hard feelings.

49.6

No new talent at the Milky Way. I don't know why we still go there, & it's not the same without Sassy B. Everyone used to ask: Hey, how's the gone girl? & I'd say she's going to e-mail, but she never did after that one message to say they'd arrived in City One. Even that was a cc to at least twenty other people. My name wasn't even top of the list. Some friend. No—that's not fair. She was my best friend. She really was. She didn't want to go, & her mum & dad made her. I mean, I WAS jealous & all that, but I'm not anymore. What's the point of moving if you leave your best friend behind?

I don't have a best friend now. Lally B keeps coming over to sit with me in Chem class but it's not the same. All she thinks about is clothes & boys AND she's got the hots for You Know Who. I told her not to bother & she sort of stuck her head on one side & said in that dim way: Oh yeah, didn't you two used to have a thing?

That Thing is OVER. I don't know what it is about him. He's just so smug now, like all the Linveki family are personal friends of the first Colonist to set foot on this planet. Since when did they have the right to get so pompous? We're all descended from the first batch, aren't we?

Moma Peg says people always do that—puff themselves up by putting other people down.

—That's stupid, I said. Other people are stupid letting them.

She laughed that big rumbly laugh. I swear the ground shook & the fountain stopped dancing for a minute.

—It's you who's stupid, Pelly D, she said—but she didn't mean it, I cd tell. I guess she's a kind of best friend now. I know she's not cool—I mean, she practically lives out on the Plaza. But she's, I don't know—beyond cool, I guess. Lots of people head straight for the fountain and the foot pools & they try not to look at her in that rickety folding chair under the cimarrons, with her cup of coffee resting on a plastic crate. Moma Peg uses the foot pools too. She has great leathery feet, so burnt they're almost black, & toenails with white half-moons. I always paint my toenails. They're pink right now. Sassy B said pink's girlie, but what does she know? She's not here, is she? Marek T does his toes too—they're copper-colored. I noticed this morning. He's probably copying Ant Li, who started the whole craze for skull stickers on the big toe. Now even Mum's doing it. I hate it when grown-ups try so hard. Why can't they just be dull & be done with it?

OK, so me n Mum are not talking right now. She won't let me have my nose pierced: says it's common.

What's the big deal? Everyone's up in the air about the gene thing & the City One drought, & all she can worry about is if her daughter has too much metal in her flesh. She only let me have the belly ring bcs I went on at her forever. Saw Ant Li checking it out—I put a red ruby ring in. He's hot but he's way Out Of Date.

I don't know why I can't just find a decent boyfriend. There are plenty of guys out there—some A1 gorgeous ones down by the docks, hauling stuff for the Beau Marine that's in Marie-Cloud's old berth. They were really fit—all bulging muscles & that. I think I like strong men. Mum says I shdn't get so hung up on physical stuff. I told her it was natural. Boy did she turn on me then—read me the riot act about what's "natural" & what's not. She's got a real thing about the whole multiethnicity issue. Says we shdn't discriminate against anyone. Except people poorer than us, of course: we're loaded, so that's discrimination, isn't it? I don't care, anyway. I like having money. Maybe I cd give some away.

50.6

Moma Peg said I cd keep my charity. I said I was only trying to help those less fortunate.

—Less fortunate? she cackles. What makes you think I'm worser off than you?

I don't get it.

3.7

Big stink at school today. Some of the final-year students organized a demo about all the workers going off to City One. They had big holo-banners flashing "STAMP OUT GENE STAMPS," & "CITY FIVE ALIVE," & "WHO GIVES AN 'A'?"

They're mad at the quotas the Atsumisi say they need to fill before they can make progress on the emergency irrigation. Something to do with building big tanks to recycle salt water. I wdn't trust that water. Salt water's foul—makes me feel sick just thinking about it. Y Bretton said in History class that people on Earth used to swim in the sea, but we've evolved beyond that. Marek T stuck his hand up & said: Why is it so good to have evolved backward, so we can't tolerate the sea like our ancestors used to? Big groan. Fortunately the bell went before they cd get into one of their endless debates. MT is clever, no one's saying he's not, only he doesn't know when to shut up. He was in the demo. I just cringed to see him there with his banner, shouting stuff against the Heritage Clan lot.

Some of the kids from established Atsumisi families are having their epigene tests done—you can volunteer for them if you haven't got anything better to do, which I most definitely have. Ant Li's really started a fad & now they're mincing around with big red-&-silver squares on their hands. They all hang out together like they're important. I thought: Baby, you got to be born with class, you can't have it stamped in your skin by a wetware machine. I'm still Queen Bee—I know what's in & what's not.

So anyway the A's got all mad about the demo & I can't believe it: MT called one of 'em a Racist. Said it right out in front of everybody. The A kid just went ape—he smacked MT in the face & sent him whammy right into the trophy cabinet. Broken plastic everywhere & MT's blood gushing down. His face went from brown to white—I swear it. V Gallesi came steaming out of her office & had Security come & break it up. I thought they'd whip MT off to the Sanatorium, but he went with another Security guy—some big bloke in uniform with an electric pacifier. Just goes to show you shdn't call people Racist. You can't go bandying that sort of word about. It's . . . I don't know what it is. I've never heard anyone say that word out loud before. It's one of those words that was supposed to be left behind on Earth, cos if you don't have a word for something how can it exist?

The good news is, we all missed our next class bcs Security wanted witnesses to e-mail statements. Instead I e-mailed Dad about it & he freaked & wrote that maybe I shd go off to the girls' boarding school in City Three instead. I'd rather die! Cooped up with a blockful of bitches, in that dire school uniform. I mailed Dad Right Back & rest assured I'm staying here at Saint-Antel's School for the Terminally Bored.

4.7

Nothing much to write. Waterworld opens next T-day. About time. I'm parched.

5.7

Nothing much happening. Dyed my hair red. Now everybody wants to. What it is to be popular.

6.7

Marek T came back to school. He's got one of those stamps. A green one. He's Galrezi! Someone asked him what had happened after the demo. MT backed off & rubbed his hand. He looked scared & I've never seen him look scared before. He usually chugs along without paying the slightest bit of attention to what people think. It's the only way he cd survive being such a loser I guess. I thought he'd be all mouthy about what had happened; you know, political—but he wasn't. Maybe Security asked him not to repeat anything. He was scratching his hand all day. We all pretended not to notice. Got my new suit ready for tomorrow—summer has finally arrived!

7.7

FINALLY!!!!! Waterworld is open for the new season! No prizes for guessing who got VIP tickets for the first night Opening. We were in the box with the Linveki family crowd but that's OK. It didn't spoil being on the receiving end of full luxury service from the Waterworld staff. I had the cutest two-piece swimsuit—cimarron yellow—with a gold hoop in my belly. A nose ring wd've completed the look, but I had to make do with rows of studs in my ears. We were right at the front of the line to go down the flumes first, & they have this great new area with bigger waves than ever before & the most offworld underwater tunnel. Yeah—I saw

Ant Li trying to catch up with me when I went through there: you've got to swim fast to catch up with me, boy-o! We gorged on the grub till I thought my suit wd pop & we about cleared the place out of Blue Mountain water. Mmmm—I love high summer. As soon as school's out I'm going to LIVE in Waterworld.

9.7

Met the gang at Ww. Usual stuff. I think Gene R likes me. He's OK.

12.7

V Gallesi in trouble—probably going to leave school. Am I HAPPY or what? She got all snooty about the new blood test—well, DNA tests actually. The Atsumisi say we're long overdue for a mapping of the intercity gene spread. V Gallesi says it's not good citizenship. Lots of the TV reporters have been saying that—freedom of ethnicity & everything. It's only for the database, isn't it? Everyone knows that there's no difference between the A's & M's & G's. You wdn't want to BE a Galrezi but that doesn't mean they're any different or any worse than others. They're creative & cultured—even the A's say that, all the time. G's have great vision. I wonder if Sassy B's mum was a Galrezi? (That wd mean she is too, right? I wasn't exactly awake through the whole gene inheritance module in Science class.) I just don't get what all the fuss is about. So the Atsumisi need more workers? There are plenty of dolts who'll do it for the extra money, right? It'll all sort itself out.

13.7

WRONG! I take that back. City One has really gone TOO FAR this time. They're sending new quotas out saying they need so many thousands of M's and G's to help. Our government was v neighborly. General Saint-Antel said they've got all the spare workers who want to leave City Five. He stated quite sternly that the gene database is nowhere near finished—from what I can tell it's hardly started. People like V Gallesi are blocking it. I read in a chat room that she's planning on taking the City Five government to court if they do compulsory stamping. It won't get to that. Nobody wants it & it's unenforceable. We argued about it in Current Affairs. I'm pleased to report that Pelly D cd hold her own on the subject. School's getting so bad—all this brain trauma over politics. Thank god for the end of the day and Ww. I'd die if I cdn't switch it all off & go for a wallow with the gang. Mum had a go at me AGAIN for coming home late.

16.7

New Security at school, all with red A stamps. V Gallesi went green around the gills—excuse the pun—I've never seen her so angry. I only know what happened bcs I was late in again (stopped off at the dealer's for some new shoes just in from a factory Overseas). VG said no way were they doing lab-rat tests in her school. Security were all smooth & oily.

—It's not lab-rat tests, they said. It's just the blood samples for DNA, it's perfectly safe.

She went off somewhere.

18.7

VG not back. The Parent-Teacher Association is furious. Dad came home from a meeting still frothing about VG letting down her responsibility to the school by getting involved in politics. He shd chill. None of the kids miss her.

19.7

VG on prime-time TV! No shots of the school, tho they did an interview with—yes, you've guessed it—Ant Li of all people. Got to admit he looked good for the cameras, but he was talking a load of rubbish—said that VG was always anti-Atsumisi. (I never heard her say anything anti-A.) Then it turns out that VG is wanted for some sort of water-meter scam—she's been getting out of surplus payments or something. I wdn't've thought it of her. Mum says it's scandalous behavior, considering what a school Head gets paid. I went into the chat room to see what the guys were saying, only the server crashed & we cdn't talk.

20.7

Server still down. No e-mail. I'll die!!!

25.7

Thank god Moma Peg gave me this diary, or I'd go crazy not being able to write anything. She said the first Colonists never had paper at all. I said, that's stupid—what happened when the Network went down or the server crashed? Exactly, she said, & that's why she gave me the diary.

Marek T looked surprised today when the latest History test results were announced & I came third in the class. I hate that speculative look he gives me. Does he think I can't be clever just bcs I'm gorgeous?

Nobody teases him in public anymore. I don't see

why he shd get extra sympathy just bcs everyone knows he's Galrezi now. I heard one woman at the shoe dealer saying we shd give the G's special consideration bcs of the way the A's go on about them. Another woman said they ought to get less not more, because they're only G's. Moma Peg says everyone shd get what they need to live well. She's probably right. I need all my money & nice things to live well.

(That was meant to be funny.)

1.8

Haven't written for weeks.

The Net's back on-line. Multiple relief. I'm having my room painted yellow. I've decided it's the IN color—cimarron yellow like the trees in Saint-Antel Plaza.

Gene R asked me out after Chem class. He's OK—I mean he's nice-looking & everything but not too well stacked in the brain department, if you know what I mean. It's one thing to play hooky from class, another thing not to be able to string a sentence together. I told him I'd think about it. A girl with my social standing can't be seen to be throwing herself away on second-rate goods. Maybe it wd be easier if we cd all get stamped, then you'd know where you stood with people. Still no resolution on the ID issue. I can't see it happening. You'd have to test thousands of people if you did all the Cities, no, tens of thousands of people. Even the hyperorganized Atsumisi at City One cdn't do that in a hurry, cd they? Don't they have their hands full with the irrigation thing?

Speaking of which—still no news from Sassy B & a funny thing happened on the Net today. I thought I'd get extra credit for History class by looking up some stuff for the next Colonial project. It was meant to be topical follow-up work on the last paper—checking out what the second-generation Colonists said about genes & DNA ID tests. They can't have been pro the idea else we'd all have stamps already, wdn't we? & we don't even have ID cards, except for personal access. Anyway, the Net was up & running fine until I did a search on the topic. Guess what—I cdn't access any of the sites. It was so weird. I know I had the right addresses cos I got them off Y Bretton—we all copied them down—& he ought to know the History sites, right? Wrong. So I checked on all the search engines, typing in various key words, and whaddyaknow—after a few failed attempts the whole computer crashed. Dad's going to go ballistic when he finds out. Mind you, Dad goes ballistic at the slightest provocation these days. He's worried about the effect the Gene Thing is going to have on business. Mum just retreats into her workshop & produces more agonized bits of sculpture that she thinks pass for Art. I might as well not have family. No one cares what I do, unless it's to stop me doing something I like.

28.8

Wow—haven't written for weeks again. It's been tense. The new Head's mission in life is to get our school licked into shape. He's a major headache. I thought the

Governors wd ride him for making our life hard—sadly no. He's a tall fella with a fat red stamp on his hand saying whoa-look-at-me-aren't-I-the-big-A? & he's got the City One lapel pin for everyone to admire. I notice he's thick with the Linveki family.

Marek T threatened to boycott school if they didn't state outright that they weren't going to implement compulsory testing & stamping. I don't know why he cares—he's had his stamp. He knows what he is. I don't know what's worse. Knowing or not knowing. As if I want one of those squares on my hand! They're not even temporary. No sign of V Gallesi. She must've been busted for whatever it was they said she'd done.

46.8

Nothing much to write this last couple of weeks. It's been the same old stuff. Mostly marking time till we can all skip school & go swimming. They're going ahead with the tests, tho—didn't really see that one coming. Mum's refusing to do it. I thought I'd refuse too. Her &

Dad were fighting well into the night. He thinks she shd go ahead & he definitely thinks I shd sign up for the school testing program. They can't make you, tho. Can they?

47.8

Another demo at school—the same Civil Liberties thing. Even I cd've told them what wd happen: they all got a trip to Security Central & they came home with pretty colored stamps on their hands. Lots of them had red A stamps, so I don't know what they were getting fussed about. Everyone knows the A's get preferential treatment. You see more & more of 'em around.

The Beau Marine came back into dock flying the City One colors. The Marie-Cloud is due back in next T-day. Can't wait. Big Bro is getting moody. Says he might as well quit school now. He shdn't, tho. That'd mean he'd have to sign up as a rating, not one of the top crew. He'd hate that.

Mum & Dad scrapping again. I snuck out & went to hang with Moma Peg in the Plaza. I took her some water & stuff & a magazine picture of the General. She really likes him—sort of hero worship. She says he once crossed the Plaza, when they opened the new East Lake, & he nodded to her & shook her hand.

—& I've never washed it since, she cackles.

—They can't make you take the test, can they? I asked.

—Why wait? she said.

Then she peeled off her dirty mitten & showed me her hand. I almost freaked. I wd NEVER have expected Moma Peg to get stamped.

—What'd you do that for? I asked.

—I've always known, sweet, she goes. I was in hospital months ago & they tested me again then. I got this stamp, so that makes me the Big A.

Wow. She's right. She's Atsumisi one hundred percent. That's so weird. I suppose I sort of thought she'd be Galrezi. You see—you just can't tell. I won't say she looked down on me after that—Moma Peg never looked down on me—but it's changed things. I've started checking out people's hands. I'm not the only one. You catch people sneaking a look, then they glance away, you know, in that hey-I-wasn't-looking-it's-all-the-same-to-me-what-color-you-are way. A group of us were talking about it after school. We had the best booth at the Milky Way & Tamsin T said: Wdn't it be OK if we just kept on not getting stamped?

—No can do, Gene R said. Everybody's gotta do it—for the database.

—I don't gotta do anything, said Lally B. Don't they know who my mum is?

Yeah yeah, we all know she can pull strings & that. But I had to come down on her side. I don't like people telling me what to do either. Don't I get enough of that at home?

—They'll find a way of getting your DNA tag sooner or later, Pelly D, said Gene R. (I'm so glad I never smooched him at Lally B's party. What a creep.)

—They can't just get your DNA, I said.

—Sure they can, he goes. They don't need your blood, you know. They cd get it from a flake of skin or from one of your lovely crinkly hairs.

He reached out to touch me but I flinched. I cdn't help it. I just had this horrible thought of guys in lab coats lurking around me, with a spatula & a test tube ready. Cd they really take hair or skin? Gene R cd tell I was mad at the idea so he carried on goading me. I hate that.

—Every time you take a plunge, Pelly D, think of all that water sloshing away into recycling. They cd find out from that.

I'm only human—it made my gills go green thinking about it. I told everyone I had to split, & went down to the canal. Sassy B wd've understood. I don't want someone doing things with bits of my body—I don't care if it's toenails or bellybutton fluff or anything. They can't have me. It's not nice. It's like people spying on you getting dressed. They shdn't know your private things. It's like people reading your diary.

Toni V pulled his fingers off the pages as if scalded. Did she mean him? How could she mean him? She didn't even know he existed. He wouldn't even have known *she* existed if it wasn't for her diary. He hadn't meant to be a spy on her.

In fact, he'd had enough of her. Absolutely enough. He didn't like reading all this stuff about Atsumisi, Mazzini, and . . . Galrezi. He felt physically sick when she mentioned the word Racist. It was disgusting—the General often said so. The General always said people should be proud of their heritage, not ashamed.

Toni V wasn't proud of anything. He used his hand

ID to pay for stuff, as credit, or to swipe him through security. Other than that he never thought about it, and he didn't see why Pelly D or anyone else should either. It was just something you had.

Angry, but not sure why, he rubbed his hand and then made a fist. The fist bunched up muscles in his forearm, so next he gave his biceps an experimental flex. Maybe Pelly D wouldn't be caught dead in dives like Supernova, but she did go on about liking strong guys with bulging muscles. After yet another week of work Toni V's muscles didn't just bulge, they ached one hundred percent. No amount of wallowing could soak away the pain. He had injections from the medic but not too often—he didn't want to get hooked on them. It happened. Some of the guys at the gym took stuff to raise the pain barrier so they could lift heavier weights. Toni V preferred to work through the pain.

As for Pelly D, she probably didn't know the meaning of the word pain. Maybe pain for her was losing a toe ring or having to fetch her own bottle of Blue

Mountain water. Pain for her would be having to swim in the pool with a loser like Kiw P.

Toni V stopped midthought and rubbed his eyes.

For all her faults, Pelly D was classy, that's what she was. Yes, totally different from the all-biceps-no-brains Demo Crew.

She was the girl who said: *Don't try—don't get.*

She was Somebody.

6.9

I'm a WRECK!

How'm I supposed to study for exams when the gene test results come back any day? They said we cd check the lists on-line, but the server's still playing merry hell. Too many people logging on, I guess. I was wondering what everyone else's results wd be. I tried to e-mail Mum, but she's still mad at Dad for submitting samples for the test & she's not coming back from the artist commune in City Four until he apologizes. I'm mad as hell too, but I don't have the option of walking out.

I did go for a sleepover at Lally B's but Dad

e-mailed them & said I had to come back. He sent Big Bro to fetch me. Big Bro didn't give me the usual lecture about obeying parental authority. I guess we're both mad at Dad. Still, the waiting shd've been over by now. It had better be soon: I'm turning into a right hag from worrying too much. I know it doesn't matter what gene tag you have—Mum's made that clear again & again like a stuck CD. It's just . . . Oh stuff it. I don't know. How can I face everyone at school if . . . Oh, it's not going to be like that. We're still Damsons, whatever else happens.

Consoled myself with a new outfit for Waterworld—it's just astoundingly cute & suits me one hundred percent. Watch out, fellas—Pelly D is down but not out!! Onward & upward!!

9.9

Got called into the San for the test results & the stamp. They didn't even give us private cubicles. Just strapped one arm to a chair & stuck one hand in a machine. It didn't hurt. That was the strangest thing. You'd think it wd hurt like mad, having that thing seared into your flesh. I guess they use a local anesthetic. A light came from the machine. I felt prickles on the back of my hand, but only like a soft kiss. Cdn't see the color. Nobody spoke. (Why didn't we refuse to go? Because you cdn't.) Pulled my hand out.

It's still here. I'm looking at it now. Don't even want to hold the pen with that hand. If I cut it off wd I bleed to death?

Green. Green for Galrezi.

Toni V refused to read the diary for several days after that.

9.9 Later

Mum came back from City Four. She swiped herself into the apartment without anyone knowing. I was home with Lil Sis. Mum came over to us on the sofa & just wrapped us in a hug. Her n Lil Sis were crying. I wasn't. I'd already done that thing. Already decided it wasn't going to get in my way. Who do the A's think they are anyway? Don't they know I'm Pelly D? I might be green, but at least I'm not a loser. I'll never be that. Mum was right. It isn't what color you are or what gene tag you have.

So everyone'll be looking? Big deal. I'm used to people checking me out. It's the burden of being gorgeous.

The bad thing was Dad's face when we all got back from school. He hadn't even checked his results by then—said it had been a nightmare, trying to keep up trade links with Overseas when the computers were so iffy. He disappeared to try & log on for the hundredth time that day. I knew what he was thinking. He'd seen the green on all our hands, even if Big Bro had his sleeve pulled down. He didn't want to be green. Well lucky for him. He's not. Looks like Mum's the green carrier in our family. Dad is one hundred percent red. He's Atsumisi. Not the dominant gene, see. Galrezi genes usually dominate A's. When you put it like that it sounds just great, doesn't it?

You know the worst thing? The relief on Dad's face. He tried to hide it but it was there for all of us to see. Then he behaved like a total loser—being all nice & telling us it was just for the database, just an emergency measure bcs of the drought.

—There's no drought in OUR city, just theirs! Big Bro screamed at him. & it's not temporary! We're stuck with these green-&-silver squares of crap on our hands!

Dad told him to go chill in a cold pool.

Big Bro raised his hand like he was going to hit him. He didn't.

I just closed my eyes. I came to my room & tried to e-mail Sassy B. Maybe she's Galrezi too.

No reply.

11.9

You know, in years to come I'm going to look back on this diary & wish I'd never started to write it. I wdn't have, either, if I'd known what heavy stuff wd be going on. I went up onto the roof with Big Bro. We'd just had a fall of rain, but Dad wdn't let us go out until it was over. I think he's ashamed of us. No one cares if we're up here, though. You can see people on the other roofs with their faces turned up to the sky—probably with raindrops glistening on their necks like me.

—Why does everything have to be so difficult? I asked.

Big Bro was moodier than usual.

—It's all changing, Pelly D, he said.

—I don't want it to change, I said. I like everything the way it was. Why does it have to change?

He gave that teenage-cynicism laugh.

—Oh c'mon, Pelly D, he said. Of course you don't want anything to change. That's bcs you, we, have it so good. Do you think everyone else has a ten-room apartment with a holo-pool & as much money as they can spend? There are kids out there who are gagging to have our life.

—They can't! I said. It's mine.

He turned & looked at me funny.

—It's not really. It's just borrowed. One day soon you're going to have to give it back.

—That's ridiculous, I said. This is our home. This is how we live.

—You know how it goes, Sis, he said. Other people want the good life now.

—They can't have it! It's mine, I said again.

—They don't care if it's yours. They don't even know who you are. They just know what you are.

He scratched his stamp, under the cloth of his sleeve. I'd never seen him quite so serious. It sort of lowered my spirits too.

—You think it's going to carry on like this? The Atsumisi making laws for everyone & we have to follow them?

Now Big Bro looked me straight in the eye—face-to-face. He was crying—a couple of tears shining.

—No, Pelly D, he said. It's not going to carry on like this. It's going to get worse.

I didn't need to know that. I wish he hadn't said it. I hate him.

12.9

First day back at school with everyone stamped. It looked like things were going to be OK. I mean, we all milled around & joked & laughed a bit. It looked like we were all going to get on with it. Everyone's had to go thru the same thing. We're not the only family with different gene tags either. Lally B's mum is Galrezi, while her dad's a Mazzini. She's an M. So who the hell does she think she is turning her nose up at my green stamp then? Oh, she thought I didn't notice but I did. Everyone's a hypocrite with their sneaky little looks. I don't hide my hand like some people. I'm not ashamed of it. It's a gene tag—it's nothing to do with me, who I am. I'm still Pelly D.

Yeah, so it looked like things were going to be OK but they're not. I didn't even make it past lunchtime. Played hooky & went for a wander. Moma Peg wasn't out in the Plaza. She does that sometimes—goes walk-about. Her plastic crates were still there & a few empty water cans. I went into a couple of dealers but I didn't feel like buying anything. (Hey, & I thought there was nothing a good old comfort-shop cdn't cure.) I came home & here I am in my room with the music turned up loud. Now that the Net's well & truly down I feel really isolated. These four walls—the fish tank—the bed—the pix of me n the gang all hanging out together. One good thing: the Head can't e-mail home to give me grief about skipping class.

13.9

Right. Today I am DETERMINED. I am NOT going to let these stupid politics get in the way of my day. I did a lot of thinking last night. I'm off to school now & I'm going to get there on time & show everyone what TRUE class is. Stuff the Atsumisi & their snooty looks. Walk down that corridor like you OWN it, Pelly D! Onward & upward!

13.9 Night

It's not official. No one says the genes HAVE to get into groups. Quite a lot of students cdn't give a damn about peer pressure & they hang out in the same old gangs. I made it quite clear that I don't think being G makes the slightest bit of difference to my social standing. Head high, Pelly D.

I gave Ant Li a classic LOOK when we passed outside the Chem lab this morning. His eyes followed me. He still wants. He still can't have. Saw something horrid, tho. One of the third-year students went to sit down at a table in the cafeteria. Everyone else at the table got up without a word & carried their trays somewhere else. No prizes for guessing: she was a Galrezi. I'd like to see anyone try that with me!!

Got home to find Mum crying again. It's all she does these days. She's so useless. It wd help if Dad didn't go on at her. They'd stopped arguing by the time I'd swiped myself in, but the air bristled. I went straight to the pool & sank underwater until Lil Sis came to fetch me for dinner. I've decided to give the comfort-shop strategy another go.

14.9

Big Mistake. Got home with my bags earlier this evening & got shouted at by Mum AND Dad this time. They were like, what did I think I was doing, spending all their money when things are so difficult?

—What's so difficult? I yelled. You said it wdn't change anything!

Dad went pink at that. He HAD said it, but he was pretending not to remember. He gave me some gumpf about didn't I know that things were going to get tight—business was falling off with Overseas.

He's lying, of course. A pretty lousy daughter I'd be if I hadn't learned years ago how to hack into his home accounts. Since he got clearance as an A he's been doing more deals than ever before. Mostly with City One & Overseas, true—not in our City—but it's all money, isn't it? I told him he shd care more about me than his money. Mum came barging in, saying he does, honey, of course he does. I didn't see Dad bothering to back her up on that one. He just put the TV on & turned the volume up. Fine. Just what we wanted to hear: more glowing reports about the new City One irrigation plan, with pictures of the big Smarm himself—General Insidian—blabbing on about the superior aqua technology. If it's so hot, why haven't they finished it yet?

Not enough workers for the glorious project—hah! I hope their gills all shrivel up & drop off. Dad's too.

Why is it that every day keeps happening like this? I KEEP putting a brave face on things. So WHY isn't it getting any better? And is it just my imagination, or are the teachers starting to go Racist? In Literacy today there were red & green & blue hands up in the air to answer questions, only somehow P Harski never noticed the greens. I even put my own hand up several times, to test the theory. Normally P Harski wd be well pleased to see his class's coolest chick bothering to join in. Today—no response. It was like he didn't even see me there.

22.9

Nothing unusual to report today. Another week of boring school & stupid people. Mind you, I did sit next

Oh my god. It's midnight now—past midnight. We've been getting hand-delivered mail—I know, archaic—& a special notice came at dinnertime, all properly signed & stamped & warranted. They want Big Bro to go to City One. He's not even Atsumisi! They're drafting lots of people from his year group. General Saint-Antel said it was a temporary emergency measure, just for the duration of the drought. Those selected get billeted in nice apartments with good water rations, apparently. They're all going to work on the aqueducts & things. Big Bro didn't get back till late. He was well pickled. We heard him fumbling with his swipe card, until Mum went to the door & let him in. He didn't even look at any of us.

—I'm not going, he said. No way am I going.

Predictably, Dad erupted.

—You'll do as you're told while you're under this roof! he said.

—Soon solve that problem, said Big Bro. I'm leaving.

Mum said: You're not doing anything of the sort. You're staying right here where you belong, with your family.

—It's an official order! said Dad, as if we were all

brain-dead. You've got to go. It's just temporary.

BB went right up to Dad & said: You stupid old man. You don't know anything, do you? I'm not going there & I'm not staying here.

They were too stupefied to stop him. He locked himself in his room—no card on Earth is going to swipe into there if he doesn't want them to. I even tried mine. Locked out too.

I knew where he was going, tho. As soon as he thought everyone was asleep, he was creeping to the front door with a backpack & a tiny glow-light. I followed him. It wasn't as easy as it looks in the movies. I know you're supposed to keep back in the shadows & not get too close, but he was walking really quickly. He didn't look back, tho. Hard heart or what? He went the long way around to the docks. Even then, he didn't go thru the main gates, like we usually do. He nipped off to the strip of dry land by the side, then clambered over the metal fence. I'm not into clambering in a big way. I went a bit farther along & found a gate. Boys are so gung ho sometimes.

It took me a while to catch up with him. He was being quiet—the other guys were the ones making noise. They were whispering, but it was that sort of agitated loud whispering & they were so caught up in what they were saying they didn't think of me. They were really leaving—the whole group of them—about eight or nine in total. They shouldered their bags & slipped through the loading bays to the canal edge.

It was hardly the Marie-Cloud—not even the Beau Marine. More of a sluggish long-distance haulage barge—I cdn't see the name or port registration number. One by one they were dropping into the water & swimming out to it. Big Bro was one of the last. He stopped to wrap his backpack in plastic.

—Hey! I said.

He whipped around like I was Secret Security or something.

—Pelly D, go home! he said fiercely.

Fat chance.

—Why are you going like this? I said.

—If you had half a brain you'd be coming with me.

—On that floating scrap heap? You must be joking.

—No joke, Pelly D. This is for real.

He touched my arm & said: I'm going Overseas & I'm going to join the O-HA. Think about it: they're one hundred percent Pro-Peace & they're the only way we're going to end this shitzer situation. I'm not going to be an Atsumisi slave worker!

—The O-HA? I shouted. They're a glorified acronym! (I at least had to try & talk him out of it.) This whole mess, it's only temporary, I said.

—No, Pelly D. You do this one thing & they'll want the next . . . & the next & the next. & each time you do the next thing thinking it'll be the last—it'll just be temporary. It's not safe here anymore!

—It's fine here! What's changed? We still go to school, don't we? We still hang out at the Milky Way. We still do everything the same.

But even as I said the words I knew it wasn't.

—Hey, Gim Damson!

Someone called out soft & low from over the water.

I said: What, you're using adult names now?

Big Bro rolled his eyes.

—We ARE adults now, Pelly Damson. We have to be.

I did the whole wait-where-are-you-going? thing, but he was already in the water.

—I'll get in touch, he said, let you know I'm all right. You should come & join me the minute you find out your name is on an Atsumisi list. Till then look after the family for me, won't you? Tell them why I had to—

—Like hell I will. Get back here on dry land!

—Come in & fish me out!

Well, he knew I wdn't do that in an outfit that cost more than his whole getaway boat. I hunkered down & rippled my hand in the water—a bit of solidarity.

—Take care, I whispered.

The water shimmied & a dark shape heaved itself up onto the barge. The ropes were already cast off.

With a low electric drone it turned and began to make its way north out of City Five.

I came straight home. There didn't seem to be any point in going someplace else. The moons were out—there were bright ripples on the pools in the Plaza. A plastic bag blew across the concrete & landed flat on Moma Peg's empty spot. Someone else not there. Wish I wasn't—here, I mean. I thought if I wrote it all down it wd make me feel better. It doesn't. It just makes it more real. Can't just wake up with everything all right again—got the words on the paper now.

Good-bye, Big Bro. Good luck.

34.9

A few more of the older kids are missing from school, I'm sure of it. Does no one else notice these things? It's probably something to do with the lists on the Big Screens in the main hall. A lot of students pretend to be excited to get the summons to City One—the Big One.

It's all bright lights there & loud music. City Five's so-o-o-o-o rustic, they say.

Yeah, we're rustic. We've got grass as green as the stamps on all our hands. You don't have to be a political genius to see what's going on here. The CCTV cameras have quadrupled in the last couple of weeks. Who's watching all the screens? Did they watch me play hooky to go to the canal—some stupid idea of seeing Big Bro come home? Did they watch me necking with Kasuko C behind the big flume at Waterworld? They shdn't be looking. Nobody else knows about it, I hope. He's a Mazzini. That doesn't mean he's not cool. Of course he is, if he's nibbling on my skin. We go to Numeracy class together. We sit near the back. It's not so bad. The A's sit in a row at the front, right in the teacher's line of fire. We have more fun in the back.

You'd think that with all the conflict going on we cd just skip school altogether. Not a hope of it. Lessons continue with the same drab regularity. It's like the worst of everything that's normal. The best things are missing. Things like just hanging out peacefully, or people just minding their own business, or Big Bro being here. I got hauled up before some Security woman about that. I was pure innocence all the way thru the questioning.

Hope they don't find this diary. They wdn't go in people's houses to look for things, wd they? Maybe I shd've written it in code—only then I'd forget the code & then I'd be totally unable to write my memoirs when I'm a gazillion years old & amazingly rich. I'll find a hiding place for it—shdn't be hard in this tip. Mum is STILL going on at me to tidy my room. I wish she'd just give it a rest—it's not like she hasn't got everything else to think about. And I've got enough problems of my own. Like will Kasuko C tell everybody about us? I don't want it to be official. He's getting all smoochy & I just want to play it cool. He asked about coming around to my house. FACT: everyone wants to come to my apartment, bcs it's just so offworld. I don't dole out the invites too often—got to keep that exclusive feel.

The other problem is Moma Peg. I think about her every time I pick up the pen to write in this diary. I asked a couple of dealers on Saint-Antel Plaza & they all just shook their heads. Where'd she go? I said. Head shake. Shrug.

Oh well. Don't dwell. Onward & upward.

35.9

What is the world coming to?! I spoke to Marek T today. It was purely accidental, let me get that straight. I blew off the big party at the Milky Way. Wasn't my thing. (Too many Atsumisi splashing about in the waterside bar.) I went snooping around the Plaza & there was MT near the cimarron grove, sitting on the plastic crates reading a book.

—Hey, this isn't Loser Central, I said.

He didn't even stop reading at first. Honestly, what are some people like? His hair was sticking up in all directions & his eyes were just thin lines. Even though it's been baking hot all week he had this long brown coat on. He kept drinking from a water bottle, some cheap non-brand, not Blue Mountain. He looked peaky—like he hadn't had a good soak in days. So I said, "Hey!" again and this time he looked up. His face sort of crinkled as he peered into the sun.

—Oh, it's you, he said.

(Oh it's you?!! Is that it?)

—Yeah it's me, I said. Glad you haven't gone blind reading that crap. What are you doing here anyway?

—Reading crap apparently.

He turned the book over & let me see it was some lame brainbox textbook—some Current Affairs thing, above and beyond any homework assignment I knew of.

—Maybe if you read a bit more you wdn't get such lousy grades, he said.

(Lousy?! I almost got an A grade in Chem class, thank you very much).

—It's called not trying & having a life, I said. As if you'd know anything about that.

He was still squinting up at me. I know I looked hot in my skintight stuff.

—What are you doing here, Pelly D? Don't you have some unbearably offworld "happening" to go to?

—As a matter of fact, I do. I was just looking for someone.

(Not that it's any of his business what I do in the Plaza. It isn't like I don't have my supercool home to go to. MT lives in one of the old blocks on the east side of the City, near the big water-treatment plants and the recycling center. It's permanently noisy from the wind farm and it smells over there too—all that chemical stuff going on.)

Then he says: Well as it happens, I was looking for someone too.

—So you actually know someone, then? Someone who actually talks to you?

—You're talking to me.

—Forget I ever spoke.

—Are you looking for the woman who used to sit under here?

That stopped me short all right.

—What do you know about her? I asked.

—Nothing really, I just wondered if that's who you were looking for. The big fat homeless woman with crinkly hair & a yellow dress?

—Her name is Moma Peg, I said. (I was bristling at the casual way he talked about her.) She's not homeless, you know. Not in a bad way, anyway. She just likes it out here.

—So you came to gloat then?

—What?!

MT swung his long legs off the boxes & stood up.

—That's what your sort do, isn't it? Have a good laugh at everyone who wasn't born with a silver spoon up their arse?

—What do you mean, gloat?

—I suppose you think the Plaza's tidier now she's gone?

—Quit talking crap. Where is she?

I cdn't tell him how desperate I felt at that point. I've

known Moma Peg ever since Mum & Dad brought me home from the lab. She's always been there, under the cimarron tree or wafting her big brown feet in the pool. & before I knew her, Mum knew her. Moma Peg gave me this diary.

—If you know something about her, I said, you'd better tell me.

He didn't come straight out with it. He looked around a bit. Then he closed his book & took a step closer.

—Look, Pelly D, I think she's gone. I think they've taken her away.

I was straight on to him about that: Don't be stupid. She's too old for their work program. & she's Atsumisi.

MT looked surprised but not totally floored.

—I didn't know she was even stamped, he said.

—Can't learn everything from books, I sneered.

(I know—cheap shot.) I didn't feel like insulting much. I wanted to know where they'd taken Moma Peg. MT was starting to look downright shifty.

—Well, there is a place . . . he started.

—What place?

—It's only a couple of blocks from here.

—Where?

—Don't you know anything about your neighborhood, Pelly D?

—Home, Waterworld, bars, dealers—what else do I need to know?

(Yeah, big bravado from the little girl. I've spent all my life in Saint-Antel Plaza Avenue & I just haven't paid attention to the, you know, unimportant places.)

MT went loafing off up the road. I thought about ignoring him. I caught up with him at the corner of Saint-Antel Plaza Avenue & Harper Boulevard.

—See that building over there? he said. He was pointing at the big sandstone building with the fancy white window grilles. I must've passed it a hundred gazillion times.

—The bank?

—It's not a bank. It's a . . . I don't know what the real word is.

—& she's in there? Is it some kind of Atsumisi barracks?

—Something like that. They call it a "hospital."

He clammed up & stalked off. What a loser. I hate teenage boys like that.

I asked Dad about the building. He said it wasn't important.

I'm tired of writing now. I'm going to bathe, then bed.

With a quick flash of memory, Toni V realized that he knew which building she was talking about. It was the one opposite the place where he got his boots mended. The soles had been cracked and he'd been thinking of trading them for a better pair, but when he saw the sign for shoe repairs he went on up anyway, and from the staircase window he'd seen that place with the white window grilles. How eerie. It suddenly brought home an idea that had been creeping into his mind for days now—the knowledge that Pelly D was real. Of course, he'd always known that she had to be real to have written the diary, only when he was just reading the words he could think of it as a story. Now he had to accept that she'd been in the plaza that he—Toni V—was redeveloping. Maybe she'd trailed her naked feet through the old-fashioned shallow pools they'd just started dismantling that morning.

It was weird to think of other people in the plaza, people probably long gone, and weirder still to be breaking their plaza apart. Toni V didn't like weird. He kept on wishing that things could be simple—just a question of flicking the safety to OFF and drilling. When you drilled, you set up reverberations of white noise and repetitive activity that dulled the brain and the muscles after a while. Hard work didn't leave much room for hard thinking. He decided that when he next read the diary he'd keep his mental safety switched to ON and not let all the talk of politics get to him. Normal people didn't mess with politics—he knew that much. That was a tough job for people like the General to worry about. Toni V had his own tough job to contend with, digging away at the faded mosaics and glazed tiles. All in all, the Demo Crew had had a long haul that summer. They had to be psyched up on morning TV bulletins and regular shots from the medic. Most of them were beyond thinking about the pools they were destroying. They just saw something that had to be pulverized and cleared up.

Toni V was tainted by images from the diary. He saw the pool as it must once have been and wished he could go wallowing himself. He wished he could have felt the Bliss in Pelly D's holo-pool. As it was, he had to be content with the quick five-minute gulp of water they got six times a shift, and the promise of a good swim after work.

Still, digging at the plaza was coming along nicely. The contractors were due in to re-lay foundations for a more modern style, with up-to-date sculptures and a high-tech public pool. The east lake had been drained and cleaned ready for fresh water. The Supervisor hadn't yet confirmed if the cimarron grove was staying put or getting the chop. Toni V hoped they'd leave it in place. Everyone liked a cimarron.

37.9

GIANT donuts for tea tonight with crunchy cimarron seed topping. Pure delish Bliss. Dad came in whistling—yes, whistling. You see what I have to put up with in this madhouse. He made me change the view-wall from deep-sea diving pictures to his favorite views of solar flares.

—Your old Dad's done good today, he says, ruffling my hair & tickling my gills.

Does he think I'm still a little kid or something? I hate it when he does that. Later I went to my room to fix my hair—you know, thinking I was going out—& HE appears in the doorway before I can hit the remote to close it.

—I want you back by seven, he says.

—Seven!! Even Lil Sis stays out later than that at the Kids' Club!

—Not anymore.

Dad really enjoyed explaining about the curfew. He could hardly stop smirking as he said, You know how things are, Pelly D. You've been watching the news.

—Hard to miss it when it's on permanently.

(I'm not kidding—I swear Dad leaves the ceiling screen on in their bedroom all night, after giving me the old Discipline 101 about not ruining my eyesight by watching it so long.)

—Hey, love, I just want you to be safe & happy, he goes.

—So less of the curfew! I said.

It's no good. The City Governors have agreed to it. So there have been a couple of miniriots?! They weren't in this part of town & Security cracked down straight off, didn't it? So there's talk of water rationing, in order to spare more for City One? It doesn't mean I have to stay put while the Milky Way is playing the sexiest tunes in town.

Oops. Apparently it does. The only consolation is that everyone's in—A's, M's & G's.

38.9

The first explosion. Vandals targeted the Test Center on Hanger Lane. Blew the whole front wall off & ruined hundreds of tests. Dad wdn't let me out to watch the firefighters & Security trying to get the Lane back to normal. I just watched TV in the pool. I've got to admit—I gloated. If only someone had blown my test results up. I swear I'll walk out of school if things get any worse there.

39.9

Turns out that the results were on-line & already logged in the main archive at City One, so the bomb didn't do any good. All the people still got their results & their stamps. Everyone's talking about it. People on the Lane are pretty shaken up by the sound of it. They figure it must've been Galrezi, so G's are not exactly welcome down there. Fine—the Hanger Lane dealers are lousy anyway.

40.9

Kasuko C hasn't said a word, thank god. We're meeting every day at Waterworld. The curfew's a pain in the bum, tho. It stays light so late, there's no chance of moonlit smoochies. Nothing much else to report. Dad got the latest sorry-can't-help from the government, about tracking Gim D. Big Bro's probably living it up in Santanna Port right now. Wish I was—specially since exams are LOOMING.

41.9

Marek T was right. Moma Peg was in that building, the old bank. I know it was mostly none of my business & not really my problem but I had to find out. OK OK, so I went AWOL from Chem class & broke into one of the staff IT rooms at school. It's the only way to get on-line in this place, I swear it. Well, I say broke in. To be fair it was dopey P Harski who didn't pull the door properly shut when he left—carrying a pile of evil-looking assignments for my class, I might add, so I had no guilt about taking advantage of his lousy sense of security.

I got on to a terminal all right. That was easy. Getting into the school files or into City facilities was impossible, even for a brainy chick like me. I may have bashed the keyboard a couple of times in frustration, but I didn't break any nails & there was no one around to see me so, hey, why shdn't I dabble in violence?

Then, just when I was probably on the brink of a genius breakthruugh, the door swipe buzzed green & it opened. I truly thought I was Toast: no amount of the famous Pelly D charm was going to sweeten up the teacher who found me this much off-limits.

So what happened?

I saw who it was, & then charm ceased to be a requirement.

—Don't you know the meaning of private, brain-dead? Why don't you just mosey on back to your hole of choice & leave the oxygen for people who count?

(Not bad for a put-down, considering the limited lead-in time.)

Marek T just gave me a dopey look & said: Charming as ever, Pelly D.

He has no right to go bandying my name around. When I'm famous I'll get it copyrighted. At least he didn't do the predictable what-are-you-doing-here? thing. He just pulled up a chair & swiveled around & around on it, watching me. I noticed he'd shaved the chin-fluff beard off. Result.

I told him where to go and what to do when he got there.

—No need to spit venom, he said. Or is Hack Queen of the Universe having a little trouble with the password?

—It just so happens that maybe I am. It is high-level security, y'know.

—Sure it is. That's why I had no trouble cracking the door code & following you in.

(He admitted to following me! The creep. I need multiple restraining orders against all the males in my life.)

—If you're so clever—

—For your information, I worked it out weeks ago, Pelly.

(Mmmm, a girl could really fall for a guy who brags like that. Not.)

—&?

—Think about it. The password's got to be something easy enough for the teaching staff to remember. & something doopy so they get a little educational thrill every time they log on.

—Well if it's something doopy I could see why you'd be the A1 candidate to figure it out.

(He walked right into that one.)

—Guess you don't want to know that badly, Pelly D, else you might try being nice for a change. It wouldn't kill you.

—What's killing me is having to share existence with losers like you.

OK, so it went on like this for a while. In the end, I had to get my priorities right. Never let it be said that Pelly D can't ask nicely when she wants something really, really badly and when the person she's asking has been sworn to secrecy. Actually, I might have spared myself the sacrifice of uttering the "please" word. I think he was getting tired of my superior wit. Or maybe he just wanted to show off. Whatever: as the password prompt box flashed up he typed in: Head for the Stars.

Yep. You read that right (even though you shdn't be reading this unless you're me). "Head for the Stars" is our inspirational motto, here at Saint-Antel's School for Oppressed Youth.

After that, the barrage of hints finally hit target & MT mooched out for whatever class he was planning on disrupting next.

The password got me into the Net at least. I did a

quick map survey of town & pulled up the info on the building I was after.

At first I thought, no big deal. It's a hospital. Then I looked for Moma Peg's name. Which I didn't actually know. I've always called her Moma Peg. Everyone does. Eventually I found her listed under Momaluke Appegee. There was a digital picture of her looking straight to camera & a profile shot with a bar code underneath. She had a medical record—with no outstanding illnesses listed, though there was something about mental problems years ago. Under current status it said, "Holding."

Why wd they be holding Moma Peg? I still can't figure it out. I shd've stayed longer—had a longer look around—but I had to sign off before anyone came to monitor. Maybe I can try again later. I'm writing this at the back of Art class. We're supposed to be drawing our hands. I did point out that I can't draw.

—Nonsense, Pelly D, came the familiar sarcastic drawl of Psycho-Art-Teacher-From-Hell. You're Galrezi—they're very artistic.

I was going to tell her not to be so Racist, but it wasn't worth it. Never look like you're having to fight your corner—people see it as weakness & it has a definite dampening effect on the Cool Factor.

44.9

Spent three hours in the pool, just watching the holograms through the water & wishing I didn't have to surface again.

46.9

I've broken up with Kasuko C. We're just good friends now and we

Oh my god! I can see it right from my window. The biggest explosion—it's making the walls shake.

Startled, Toni V leaped down from the bunk, landing straight on Monsumi Q, who'd fallen out of bed with shock. He ran to the door to join a group of lads who were already crowding at the big stairwell windows.

"Will you look at that baby go down!' Hood N whooped—in the front, as ever.

There was a second explosion of sound and the apartments shook again. Night blasting had started in an attempt to keep on target with the rebuilding program.

Toni V pushed his way to a window to get a better view. "Looks like they're pulverizing the whole block," he said.

"They are. Wait for it . . . *Bang!*"

They all cheered as the next lot of explosives was detonated.

Only Mon Q was gloomy. "What d'you bet we'll all be detailed for rubble-clearing duty once the dust has settled?" he said, chewing the end of his long bangs.

"I hope not," said Toni V, watching the dust cloud rise into the twilight air. "Clogs the gills up, makes your eyes gritty."

"You're just in love with that big yella drill of yours," said Cred N. "I've seen you get all delicate with your drilling."

"Like it's his girrrrlfriend," Hood N jeered.

"I'm just careful," said Toni V. "I don't want to damage anything."

He realized straight off how stupid that sounded. Since when could a digger dig without damaging something? It wasn't really the time to tell them about Pelly D and her diary in the water can. If he said: *Dig—dig everywhere*, the gang would probably take that as a go-ahead to drill up the whole town, so instead he whooped and cheered along with everyone else.

Hood N crowed louder than the rest of them. “Man, that’s one hell of a reverb! Can you feel the walls shake?”

Toni V actually had to put his hands out to steady himself, all the while wondering what would it be like to wait for bombs to fall or missiles to plough into the side of your apartment; wondering if the explosion that Pelly D heard had been from a missile, and if so, was she okay? At this point he realized how muddled he was in his head: he was thinking about the diary as if it was dealing with things that had just happened, when in fact . . . in fact he didn’t know how to think about it. He preferred not to think.

He forced himself to stay watching the demolition until the last building went down and the dust cleared. When the Block Leader came to hustle them all back to their bunks, the last thing Toni V heard was Hood N’s jubilant, “God, it’s good to be alive!”

3.10

Mum said take only essentials & valuables.

Everything's essential & valuable! This is all just totally ludicrous! I can't believe I'm even sitting here writing this.

She's given me the most minuscule bag ever & says that's all I can have for now. It'll about fit my skimpiest swimsuit. Why can't we just pack everything & have it sent over to the new place? Bcs. Bcs of the crappy new rules that say City Five has to be properly multiethnic. That people shdn't hoard. Well, all they had to do was ask. I wd've given my stuff away much more readily. I always take last season's clothes to the vintage dealer. I recycle everything. Why do I have to leave my stuff behind? Dad says we cd always collect some more later if Security aren't being too watchful. Lil Sis is crying in her room next door. She can't decide which toys to pack. She wants to be glad she doesn't have a shoe collection like mine. Oh stuff it. I'll tell her she can fit the brown iguana in my bag, since it won't go in hers.

I said to Dad: Oops, won't be able to fit any school books in, best not go to school anymore.

—Don't be so lippy, said Dad. Take all your books to school & leave them in your locker. You're not moving till tomorrow night.

TOMORROW NIGHT! Doesn't he realize how ridiculous that is? I bet even Big Bro took more stuff in his backpack. Too bad he didn't take a letter-writing kit, bcs we STILL haven't heard a damn thing from him. Maybe he signed up for the wrong boat when he got to the coast & ended up close to the fighting, tho I don't think so. The nearest City is City Two & it's a good 100K away. No, I bet our heroic Gim D's just forgotten all about us, he's so busy being about to save the world with the O-HA. Wonder what it's like Overseas, apart from the rain and snow. It's got to be better than the situation here right now. I heard on the news that the ferry routes westward, between here & City One, are being blockaded & the land all around is turning into a regular War zone. Terrorists—god do I wish they'd left that word behind on Earth, too—terrorists are setting off more bombs like the one I heard four days ago.

At least Cities Three & Four are doing OK. Just OK. They're not doing well . . . Lots of refugees are heading to us—big, welcoming City Five-Alive-O! Which is why the General says we all have to share & share alike. Or, to be more precise, the Galrezi have to give up their posh apartments & move into the so-called Artists' Quarter. South side of the Plaza—ugh. Mum's vaguely excited about it, I can tell. She doesn't seem to mind that Dad's going to stay & babysit the apartment until all the "sharing out" is done. Things between the two of them have gone so downhill they cd set up a ski resort. Mum's tried to play it down. Dad just keeps gabbling on as if everything's normal. It isn't so bad for him—his business is doing really well. I think he likes being Atsumisi because it makes him feel important. I heard Mum yelling at him one night to get his priorities right.

She says the new block we're going to is home to some of the best artists & craftworkers in the City. Maybe they'll lend her some clay bcs she certainly isn't taking her workshop if I can't take my entire music collection.

The irony is, the new block is exactly opposite, on the far side of the Plaza. I can just about see the windows from my window now. I never cross the Plaza to that side of town. How nice. It'll all be new & exciting for me, won't it?

Oh, I can't stand it. It's all so—so OUTRAGEOUS.

My last night sitting at this desk writing this diary. Might as well make the most of it. There's always something to say.

Security's tighter after the second bomb last month—the one I thought was a Direct Hit on our apartment.

(Soon to be someone else's apartment . . . Why does sharing & neighborliness mean someone else gets our apartment? Or maybe it means that after they've had it for a while they'll have to "share" it back again with us.) Boy, was that ever an explosion. The TV cameras were on to it straightaway. General Insidian says they'll have to send more Security if Atsumisi lives are threatened by vandals. Three people did die in the explosion—all Security: two M's & one G, as it happens.

I didn't get so long in the IT room at school today this time around. I checked Moma Peg's file again. Her status was blank. I tried to skip out of school, but Security on the main entrance wdn't let me & all the fire exits now have locks that only open if the Head overrides them. They're going to install a new sort of swipe at the main entrance too, so all the students AND teachers have to have their stamp "read" as they come into school, or leave. It's to keep tabs on people while the vandals are disrupting City peace, apparently. I've got to say, I've gone beyond believing the things they tell us now. The Big Screen in the school hall is set to 26/7 news & we all have to watch during Assembly. No getting away from it. The TV's always droning on about work quotas & peacekeeping.

So anyway, about Moma Peg. I had to wait till after school. I said I'd meet the gang at Waterworld, but I had to do some shopping first. Cheerio gang. I went to the "hospital" instead. They had a new ID swipe on the door. I sort of hustled in after a group of nurses. Reception pulled the file for me.

—Is she here? I asked. Can I see her?

The woman on Reception went all sad-faced on me.

—Sorry, love, she said. M Appegee is no longer with us.

I was unstoppable!

—Look, I said, she's a . . . a kind of aunt, and her family wants to know she's OK. Can't you tell me where she is?

The receptionist had a soft face.

—Come back in ten, she said. I'll see what I can find.

When I got back she wasn't so soft.

—Let me check your stamp a moment, she said.

One view of my green-&-silver had her reaching for the Security button under the desk. I told her not to be so alarmist. I told her who my Dad was. I told her he was Atsumisi. It really stuck in my throat to "boast" like that. It sort of worked. She didn't buzz for Security. She didn't tell me anything about Moma Peg either. How'm I supposed to find out what's happened to her? What if she needs to get a message to someone—to me—& they won't let her contact anyone? Maybe she's got her own diary she's writing in? I doubt it. Moma Peg was never the writing type—probably why she passed this notebook on to me. So if she can't write, how are we going to know? I loitered for a bit, feeling fish-out-of-water. Didn't dare to speak to anyone leaving. Coward.

3.10 Midnight

The saga continues. Net connection is up & running again! It's been on all evening (Dad didn't see fit to tell me)—our last evening here. Mum had a row with Dad about it. She said the b*****ds had only re-established the server bcs they thought all the Galrezi were out. Dad said don't be paranoid.

I logged on to e-mail straightaway. Nothing. I mean it. Nothing. When in the history of electronic mail did anyone ever have an empty in-tray? My files were empty too—all my address book was wiped. If I hadn't used up all my store of furiousness stomping around "packing" I might've been madder than a mad thing. As it was, I went straight to the hospital home page. Moma Peg's file was wiped too. No forwarding address. Moma Peg wasn't big on addresses anyway. At least once she gets out of That Place I'll still be able to mosey on over to the cimarron on the Plaza & see what was going on with all that "hospital" crap.

Moma Peg's got her head screwed on right. She wdn't get all sniffy just bcs she's Atsumisi & I'm Galrezi. She always told me you don't puff yourself up by putting other people down & you look at a person's inside before you check out their outside. I never particularly listened to her of course. I was young then. At least I remembered. I can try that way of looking from now on. There isn't going to be much else to do in the new apartment. I bet they don't have a holo-pool or wall-to-wall TV, or customized view screens. Still, the three of us will be together, that's the main thing & Dad can let Big Bro know our new address when he sends a message to our proper apartment. I don't see why we can't all wait at the new place until this "sharing" thing is sorted. Mum says it doesn't work like that—we were lucky to get a three-bedroom apartment as it was. There's a waiting list & Dad had to pull a few strings, call in a few favors, blah blah & blah. Dad claims he has to stay on the north side of the Plaza bcs of business contacts. Mmm, & we're really convinced by that one. Truth is, he's embarrassed to live with us. I see his eyes flicking to our green stamps. Lil Sis is having the worst time of it. She knows something's wrong but she's too young to have things explained to her properly. She cuddles up to Dad a lot. He half cuddles back. I bet he's going to love having our beautiful holo-pool to himself. I can't lie—I hate & despise the man.

So, my last night in this bed. Consolation prize: the new place is farther from school, so I'll get fitter walking there in the morning, so I'll look cuter than ever in my new yellow swimsuit. See how I look on the bright side. G'night—sweet dreams, Pelly D.

4.10

It's no big deal at school about the new apartment. People all over the City are having to move, so I don't stand out like a bad fashion mistake after all. I got a couple of invites to housewarmings. Ant Li has a new apartment. Well waddyaknow, it's even better than the one they had before, tho only seven rooms. Wonder if they put in to get transferred to our old apartment? Somebody lucky is going to get it eventually. I hate them already. One of the Linveki companies has won big contracts for some pipeline or other, so they've gone supernova with the old didn't-we-do-well smirks. Overseas, they've also won a contract to build a new dam—it's supposed to be the "Glorious Revolution of Hydropower," have you ever heard so much garbage before in your life? It just means more workers have to get shipped across the ocean to slog for the Atsumisi. Or, thinking about, it could mean that this water-hostility business cd soon be over & done with, if they set up purification plants in the dam to make sure there's enough good water for everybody. Hey, if there's enough water & if all the politics would just stop, I cd get on with far more important things in life: I've got some SERIOUS socializing to catch up on!

Somehow I don't think I'll be hosting the galaxy's most-sought-after sleepover parties at our new place. The truth is, I wanted to die the minute I saw the block. The lifts were broken—surprise surprise. The door swipe was jammed, so we had to use a manual lock. And it is TINY! Only three bedrooms & a weird sort of carpeted living area with a sunken foot pool in the middle of the floor. Very retro. No kitchen: it's all communal cooking in big kitchens in the basement. Yes, the basement. The only pool in the building is on the roof. Yes. On the roof. It collects rainwater. How back-to-nature. As soon as I saw the place I nearly walked right back out again.

Mum caught me by the collar.

—You'll stay right here, girl. This is the best of the lot, & we'll just have to make it nice, won't we? See—can you hear that flute playing from next door? I told you it wd be an artist's paradise.

I closed my eyes. No good. It was all still there. I took Lil Sis into her box—I hesitate to call it a room when it doesn't even have a personal hot pool, or a TV even. We set her toys out on the bed there & played a game that involved hiding her dingy iguana up my designer shirt. Lil Sis is easily pleased. She even thought it was great fun, having to get a tray & wait in line at the kitchen. Enough said. If I haven't died of claustrophobia by the end of the week then I might just have the heart to unpack. Dad sent some proper food over: donuts and milkshakes. Mum said we'll just have to send out for a lot of take-out food until we get settled & Dad'll keep sending us crates filled with Blue Mountain bottled water. Hope he remembers I like cherry flavor best.

At least we've got money. Some of the people here look like they haven't had a job since they were born. I keep forgetting that Mum actually makes money from her pottery stuff. Or used to. Everyone's into Big Hero sculptures these days.

I won't even begin to write about my bedroom. In fact, I can't write about it. My pen, my hands & this diary have melted bcs there's no air-conditioning. Here I go—a pool of hot goo on the floor.

The cimarron trees stayed. Word came from somewhere close to the General himself that the trees were to be incorporated into the new design. Toni V only found that out when he overheard a couple of the other guys talking in the line for the midday water break. The sun was directly overhead and the whole plaza shimmered. It should've been pretty, but it only made his eyes ache. It reminded him of the big concrete play area by his old school, where the only shade came from the diamond pattern of the wire fence. He much preferred the gentle shimmer of the sky seen from underwater. Who wouldn't?

So the trees stayed and the work continued.

Then came the sound that Toni V had half been waiting for: a shout and a buzz of excitement. One of the Demo Crew was breaking up a patch of ornamental slabs about two hundred paces away from the cimarrons, toward the center of the plaza.

The Supervisor slid out from his spot in the shade and walked over. He had one hand over his eyes, squinting to see what all the fuss was about. "Quit shirking!" he yelled. "Shirking's for losers!"

For the rest of the crew, it was a question of keeping one eye on work and one eye on the disturbance. Most people thought there had been some kind of accident and were watching for the medic. Toni V knew better. Hadn't the shaky blue writing said: *Dig—dig everywhere*?

A wooden box was uncovered—valuable in itself. Inside, as he found out later, was a hoard of money, some silvered photograph frames, share certificates in a very up-market Overseas trading company and a jumble of top-quality jewelry.

"I was just digging when I saw it! Another bit to the left and I'd've totaled it!" The man who had found it was a veteran—the sort of man who had dust ingrained in every wrinkle, and more calluses than skin on his hands. Looking at him, Toni V saw himself twenty years from now, still demolishing and rebuilding. Surely the work would be done before then? Surely things would be back to normal again soon, like the General promised.

The Supervisor quickly bagged and tagged the find. "Okay, fellas, gawping is for losers. *'Back to Work—Back to Normal.'* I'll see this gets to the proper authorities."

That evening in the pool Toni V didn't feel the Bliss as usual. He just felt tired. His eyes ached more than ever, and his foot didn't seem to be healing properly. He'd tried to work out at the gym. Tried and failed. His muscles had rebelled and it had been all sweat for nothing. He got to the pool pretty late. It wasn't too full. Hood N's waterball team was horsing around in the deep end, playing some sort of diving game.

Toni V submerged, hoping this would take his mind

off things—things like Pelly D. He turned and rolled lazily near the bottom, finally getting a good buzz of oxygen. At the far end of the pool, the water was churned up like a feeding frenzy. The guys had someone stuck down there, someone thrashing about. The water frothed with bubbles.

Alarmed, Toni V cut through the water and hauled the prey up. He got thumped and kicked a lot before he made it to the surface, dragging a limp Kiw P after him. Toni V trod water angrily for a moment, then pulled Kiw P by his chin to the side of the pool. The kid's blond curls were plastered flat over his face and his neck scars looked worse than ever.

Toni V had no idea what to do next. He got out of the pool and tried to heave Kiw P out too. The movement set the unconscious body coughing—spraying water and worse onto Toni V's leg. Kiw's eyes opened. He flipped over onto his stomach and threw up some more. Toni V scrambled to his feet and backed off.

Hood N wasn't far away, bobbing about in the water

with his mates, all sleek brown muscle and generous smile.

"Hey, Toni V! Don't freak. We were just having some fun."

"Some fun." Toni V was surprised to hear the sound of his own voice. People never talked back to Hoodie.

"Oh, we wouldn't've gone too far."

Toni V looked down at Kiw P, who was feeling around for a towel and planning a quick escape. "You shouldn't do that to him. You know he can't . . . *you know.*"

"Aw, you his mummy?" one of the waterball team cackled.

Toni V wished all the waters of the world would pour through the ceiling and wash him away—anything other than get lumped with the runt. But he stood his ground. He suddenly understood what Pelly D meant by people who puffed themselves up by putting other people down.

Then Hood N was at his side, with a friendly arm

around his shoulders. "Look—no hard feelings, Toni V. You did good then for the no-gill guy. Me 'n the gang, we get a bit high spirited, y'know."

He didn't know.

Hood N tried a different tactic.

"I heard the Demo Crew has been poaching on our turf—you found something . . ."

Flushing with alarm, Toni V tried to stammer a denial. Then he realized what Hoodie meant.

"Oh, yeah. Today. A box with stuff."

"Nice. Are you getting your cut?"

"No! The supe has it."

"Shame. You missed out there."

"Isn't that against the—"

"Rules and Regs? Yep. Us guys on the Salvage Squad consider it one of the perks of the job. And let's face it—it is a pretty perky job. You should think about switching over. I could use someone good on my crew, over at Hanger Lane."

Toni V wanted to be righteous, he really did. He

wanted to stand up for what was "right." The trouble was, Hood N was one of those vibrant people who could charm water from a stone—or in this case, a smile from the sullen. Hood N wasn't bad. It was like he said himself—he was just buzzing on "high spirits." So Toni V didn't stalk out of the pool room. He hid his awkward pleasure at even being noticed by someone in the Salvage Squad and said, "I . . . I don't think my supe would let me go."

Hood N unsnaked his arm and slapped Toni V on the shoulder instead.

"Leave your supe to me, Toni V. Later, then."

"Later."

Hood N dived flawlessly into the pool. It looked like Bliss.

Toni V dived in after him—but not before catching sight of Kiw P mouthing a silent thank-you from the doorway.

He told Monsumi Q and Credula N about it later. "What do you think, guys?"

"It's only Kiw P," said Cred N. "They were just horsing about. And, hey, if Hoodie N can get you a transfer to salvage you're made!"

Mon Q looked thoughtful. "I suppose they ought to have been more careful. There'd be a big stink if anything happened to the kid."

"And he might have been hurt," said Toni V, feeling idiotic.

Cred N shrugged, but Mon Q slapped Toni V on the shoulder. "You did the right thing. Kiw P's not a bad sort . . . even if he is a freak."

It seemed like a good opening to talk about other things—about the diary—but Cred N was off and away doing his Kiw P drowning impersonation.

10.10

I've survived the first week in this new squat, but—disaster! Can't find my nice pen—the lucky pen. Must've left it at school. I'll never see it again now. People are getting really sneaky. Funny, isn't it, how my pen has gone off to have a life of its own & no one'll ever know that it once belonged to the great Pelly D? (Unless they know me & swiped it off my desk during History today. In which case they ought to be shriveled up with shame. My pen ought to blot in their hands; it ought to run out of ink. Explode.)

I borrowed a crayon off Lil Sis. In return I have to play with her for a gazillion hours while Mum does her stint in the communal kitchen. Bring back my life of pampered indolence! Come back luxury! I'll appreciate you even more now I've had to live in this slum for a whole eight days.

A girl from my year is in the apartment across the hall. We sometimes walk to school together. Her name is Hanna S. Her family's pretty sloppy. Her mum & dad just call her Hanna. There are six of them in a two-bed apartment. Looks like the whole family has the guilty epi-gene lurking away in their chromosomes. Hanna S isn't my best friend or anything. That's still Sassy B, even if she is living it up in City One as I write. (I bet she doesn't have to swat insects before going to bed. Mum's stretched a piece of fine cloth over the window so I cd sleep with it open & not get bitten to death by the ascis. These little pests-on-legs come up from the canals to feast on people instead of . . . of whatever the hell they eat when they can't suck my blood. Nice of Mum to be a sweetie for a change. I suppose she cd be a lot worse. It's not her fault that the whole world's gone gene-crazy.)

I went up to the roof pool & I'm not the only one with an offworld suit. All us rich kids are looking at each other. No one likes to say anything out loud. If we'd started saying things out loud we might've ended up screaming.

The apartment shrinks every night. It's true. The walls are slowly creeping in. There's barely enough room for a bed & a chair in this room as it is. I have to store all my clothes in a DIY cupboard next to the window. Mum's room has an en suite toilet & shower & bath. She's been letting us use it, tho. I miss our POOL!!! All those glass shelves with pamper products! The mountains of freshly laundered towels! OK, so we've still got towels here. They're looking a bit gray. We don't send them out to be cleaned anymore. We have to take them down to the basement to go in one of the machines there. Lil Sis n I do this job. She likes to put the tokens in the machines to make them go. Little things amuse little minds . . . When we're done telling the tale of how we picked her up from the lab & brought her home, we just sit & make up stories about the other people in the basement. I wonder what their real stories are.

Dad's going away on a business trip—he sails on

the Beau Marine along the coast westward to City One. I asked if I cd go with him, he said: No sweetie, you've got your exams. Looks like the Bright Lights Big City thing will have to wait until this mess is over & the exams too. He came to our new apartment to say good-bye. Mum refused to speak to him. I think I'd've preferred it if she'd just yelled at him.

11.10

Got to start writing smaller. I'm halfway through this diary already. I never thought I'd write so much. We still have the laptop, so I cd do a diary on that, only I don't trust the electrics in this place. When there's a break in the evening news you can watch the apartment lights flicker & dim as everyone goes to put the kettle on. I can hardly believe this is just the other side of the Plaza from our lovely lovely home. It's another universe here. Thank god for Waterworld. I bathe & shower there, as well as doing all the pools & flumes & bars. A girl's got to have some fun.

12.10

Back in my room alone. Really shaky. The sky is orange. The lamps on the Plaza are mostly out—smashed in the demo. I can smell the smoke even through double glazing. Just small fires—nothing dangerous. Not to us at any rate. The caretaker pulled big metal grilles over the main entrance. We all had a bird's-eye view—well, as much as anyone cd see in the semidark.

How did everyone else know there was going to be a demo? The staff at Waterworld said it wd be safer to go back home—Security was letting everyone know there wd be trouble. I don't understand that. How cd they know there was going to be trouble before there was any? The crowd looked pretty peaceful to me. They were mad all right—that bit I do understand. They had all the usual banners: "CITY FIVE ALIVE" & "SAY 'NO' TO DISCRIMINATION" (they almost cdn't fit that one on the board). As far as I cd tell, the people were just milling around—saying hi & getting the feel of things. I skirted the whole Plaza. I think part of me wd've liked to lose myself in the crowd. Most of me just wanted to get home safely. I took one of the leaflets, tho. Does that make me a subversive? I tried to see who was in the demo.

It was funny—some people were going around with a green spray, coloring in everyone's hands. After a while you cdn't see what color the stamp was. It didn't make any difference, tho. Security had the whole Plaza ringed before nightfall. I never knew there were so many Security officers. They can't have drafted them from other cities—there are demos in Cities Two, Three, & Four, tho the TV calls them riots. I recognized one of the Security guys—Kasuko C's big bro. I said hi to him & asked what was going on. He said the Galrezi were kicking up a stink for no reason & that the Security were just brought in for peacekeeping. I kept my hand out of sight. In a way I was pleased he assumed I'd be Atsumisi or at the v least Mazzini. & in a way I wanted to smash my green fist into his square-jawed face.

I got home OK, which is something. G's are more likely to be detained if they're stopped & questioned—

that's a fact. Lil Sis & I sat on the front windowsill, hoping to see the TV cameras. That's how we know what happened. After a while I made Lil Sis get down & go to bed. She didn't want to, but when Mum's working she's got to do as I say. Besides. It's not good for a six-year-old to see things like that.

Security had rubber truncheons first. They didn't start firing into the crowd until a bit later on. They weren't real bullets. They wdn't use real bullets. Big Bro once said that in olden days, on Earth, Security used to use water cannons. That doesn't work with us, of course, tho it wd be a better way to break up a demo—the crowd wd all be too happy to care about issues, if they were being sloshed with cool fresh water on a hot dry night. As it was, people started screaming. I don't blame them. Most tried to get away. The crowd was a big dense blob, stretching out into surrounding streets. There were too many people. There must have been a few thousand. Security on horseback herded them back to the Plaza. People started throwing things. I saw one of the first lights go out. A woman threw a sandal—she just bent down & slipped it off, then lobbed it as hard as she cd at one of the Security. She missed & hit the light instead. She was obviously a trendsetter—soon everyone wanted a go. There are still some shoes left on the Plaza, along with dead banners & placards nobody's going to hold anymore. It's like footage from the old days on Earth. I thought the reason people traveled light-years to Home From Home planet was to get away from all this sort of nightmare?

The TV said it was all over peacefully & that no one was hurt. That isn't true. People were fighting like savages right till the end. I saw them—kids my age as well as adults—battering away at the gray Security uniforms, smearing that green dye everywhere. Ambulance crews came silently. They pulled bodies away & the demo was over. I closed the blinds & sat in the dark.

I don't want anyone to know I was watching. My swimsuit's still in the bag, wet. I haven't dried my hair or even brushed it. Water's trickling down my neck & onto this diary. I don't care. Nothing's going right. I'm going to try and stay awake till Mum gets in. Hope

Dad's OK on the other side of the Plaza. Hope Big Bro's OK wherever he is.

17.10

There haven't been any more demos this week. The City's pretty peaceful, apart from one or two minor flare-ups. Everyone you meet says it's best not to kick up a fuss. We don't want trouble in the City. Or worse—some kind of civil war. General Insidian has issued a statement saying he hopes people won't put their wellbeing in danger by rioting against the governments. (Which wd be nice if City One hadn't just published a paper on the Net "proving" that Galrezi make a less-valued contribution to society than Atsumisi & Mazzini. Cheeky b*****ds.)

Despite all that, the general feeling seems to be that everyone just has to calm down. Going down the street you look at people & it's like we're all being on our best behavior. It's just like I said—the Colonials didn't travel a gazillion light-years to found a new Home & then start squabbling over it.

Apparently, people are going to big Guidance meetings about the early ideals of the Colony. We had one at school—lots of speeches about living in harmony & not making life difficult for your neighbors. All well & good, except that it seems the Galrezi are getting blamed for all the demos! Security ran scans of the crowd & reported that the majority of protestors were G. (Well, YES! Naturally—they've got the most to protest about.) There were a couple of hundred A & M too, but the G's were a huge majority. So now OUR government's saying that G's have a responsibility to themselves & the City. Apparently, it's up to US to make sure that no more public property gets vandalized, & that no one else gets hurt in a crowd. I like that!! I suppose that means the Galrezi just made those Security guys pull the triggers & thwack the truncheons?

I'll answer my own question. I can, bcs the TV's told me everything I need to know about the current political situation. Fact is, the Galrezi provoked Security. Yep. They behaved aggressively, & we've all had it drummed into us just how evil aggression is, haven't we, boys & girls?

Major exams still looming. What a nice distraction. I don't know how I'm expected to study in this dump, with riots outside & Lil Sis singing next door. The Head just announced a special prize for Galrezis—for outstanding contributions to Art in school. How nice. Mum says I shd enter the competition. She must be ill. How can she say that when she's seen how badly I draw? She's started saying stuff like, I shd be proud of my Galrezi heritage, & it's obviously what makes her such a good artist, blah, blah, blah. No point in trying to tell her I just want to stand at the helm of the Marie-Cloud & steer her off to some freshwater paradise. Anyway—drawing & arty stuff is Right Out as far as my future career's concerned.

To prove her point, there was a blotchy doodle in the margin of the page—a stick figure with long dark hair, big eyes, and pouty lips. Toni V stared at the picture as if it was some strange species scared out of its natural habitat by explorers in the New Frontier.

So this was Pelly D.

She'd become very vivid in his mind. After pages and pages of random life story he had somehow lost track of the fact that she existed somewhere apart from in his head; she was as real as the diary in his hand. In a way, he was glad it was only a scribble picture, not a photograph. There was part of him that didn't want to face up to the truth that all he had of Pelly D was her diary. Looking at her photo would only prove how unobtainable she really was. He was already beginning to understand that the war had come between them, though if anyone had asked why this made him feel uneasy he couldn't have said, specifically. There were some thoughts he didn't have words for yet.

In his mind Toni V thought he knew what Pelly D looked like—the gorgeous glamour girl who keeps you awake for weeks on end and who doesn't even notice your existence. Every time he saw a girl near the plaza, or on one of the avenues, Toni V stared, wondering if any of them knew Pelly D.

From scraps of information in the diary he had been trying to work out where she lived—both the posh apartment and the apartment they were moved into under the new "sharing scheme." It was hard for him to sympathize with her move to a smaller place. He'd grown up in a four-walled box pretty much, with three sisters and a series of stepdads—not exactly the lap of luxury, like Pelly D. He'd grown up quickly, learning to get on with whatever he'd been set to do, and to keep out of trouble. He supposed it must have been harder for Pelly D to "go down in the world" because she'd always been so "up" in it, whereas he'd started down, so the only way was up. At least, that was the case if you subscribed to Pelly D's philosophy—onward and upward.

This sort of ambition didn't sit well with everything else Toni V had learned growing up, everything he knew from the Rules and Regulations. The more Pelly D rippled through his mind, the more he tried to still himself and keep steady. Then, maybe a week after seeing the doodle, Toni V got plunged right into one part of Pelly D's world.

Someone suggested winding down at Waterworld.

A cousin of a friend of a cousin had a group ticket and no one would be crazy enough to pass up the chance to go. This sudden connection to Pelly D created an irresistible temptation to read on.

21.10

It had nothing to do with exams! I don't know why we bothered discussing it. Some wiseass said they were late for History bcs they twisted their ankle on a broken paving slab. Y Bretton thought he'd be clever & open up the topic—how shd people get around in the Cities? He suggested cars & obviously got hooted down. Who's going to be mad enough to fold themselves up into one of those archaic boxes? Besides, where wd they all go? Gene R said what's wrong with walking, since it's what everyone does already. So Y Bretton asked, don't we have a duty to evolve and use technology, as long as it's done responsibly? Tamsin T suggested more boats. I don't think it wd be such a bad idea to have a network of public waterways right across the City, as well as the transport canals. Very romantic, cruising along, with a handsome fella at your side . . . If they dredged deep enough waterways, we could have the Marie-Cloud sail right up to school in the morning. Y Bretton took it one step further & suggested swimming to school. We were just having a giggle at the idea of waterproof textbooks when Marek T just erupted—leaped up to his feet & swept his books onto the floor. His face was all twisted with anger—worse than I've ever seen anyone.

—How can you do this? he shrieked. How can you all sit there as if this is perfectly normal when the world's breaking up all around us? I can't stand it anymore!

—Apparently not, said Y Bretton, in his dry voice. Perhaps you'd like to see the school Medic?

—What, & get carted off to the Hospital of No Return—no thank you!

A couple of students cheered when he left. I didn't. Talk turned back to the possibility of extending the intercity ferry system.

I met Marek T later, when I was coming back from a real damp squib of an evening at Waterworld. I bumped into him on Orelia Avenue, just at the turnoff to Hanger Lane. He practically threw his take-out burrito all over my sandals. I'm not good at lying. I told him he looked awful, then I asked him where he got the cut on his forehead.

—At the demo, he said, all macho & defiant. & you look as perfect & unruffled as ever, he said.

I just rolled my eyes & asked why he didn't run home to Mummy. He looked away.

Great. So it turns out that both his natural parents died years ago. How cd I have known that? So he lives with a guardian. Correction, LIVED with a guardian—apparently the guardian, a Mazzini, got called up for work in City One. MT was told to leave his apartment bcs it was too big for one person. They arranged for him to go to the Youth Barracks. Just a temporary measure until he gets somewhere better.

I said: How nice for you. He said: Don't be dumb.

HE called ME dumb?!

—It's temporary till my name comes up on the work quotas, he said. Count yourself lucky that they're doing males first, working their way through the alphabet.

Then he said: Hey, don't worry about me, Water Baby. You just go on home to your fancy apartment & your holo-pool—yeah, I heard about that.

—Enjoy your barracks, I said, not seeing why I shd tell him about our move.

—I'm not going back there, he said. Too much CCTV. They monitor everything. I've been sleeping rough.

That really p****d me off. I had visions of him camping out among the plastic crates in the cimarron grove, in Moma Peg's place. Only the crates have all been cleared away now, just like Moma Peg. Wd they clear MT away too? Diary, I've got to tell you: I said a crazy thing next . . .

So what did he say in reply?

—Live with YOU? he blurts out.

—Excuse me: volume! I said.

He was practically yelling his head off.

—I'm not a charity case!

So how come when you try & offer people good stuff they go all mad on you? Like when I offered Moma Peg money from my own savings account. Obviously she thought she'd be all right with her red stamp. But they got her, too. For what? Being untidy. No kidding—that's a crime these days. Security is big in the City. Me n Lally B got frowned on just for giggling & messing around outside the ice-cream bar. As if we were bothering anyone.

Anyway, there's Marek T going "I'm not totally down and out," and there's me, just GOING, period, when who shd turn up but the great Ant Li himself, complete with posse. Some one shd clean out the

Linveki water tank bcs this creep was just OILY.

—What's this? he smarms. The great Pelly D lowering herself to talk to scum on the street?

I told him where to go stick his head & what to cram in his gills.

His face changed. I can hardly bear to write what he said next—the B*****D. He said: Oh, I forgot, now you're Galrezi it isn't really lowering yourself anymore, is it?

Too stunned to speak. Stormed off, shoving MT out of the way.

Fine—that's what I get for being neighborly. Automatically walked to the Plaza—Moma Peg's always the person I can go to when I'm out of the loop. Deserted. A couple of newspapers flapping around, the thin plastic all crinkled & faded from the sun. Sat on the edge of the public pool, flipped off sandals & dangled feet. Didn't want to get in. Water none too fresh. Someone came up. Freaked a bit—thought it was Security. Worse. It was MT again: big bruise on the side of his face & a swollen lip.

—What happened to you? I asked, not really bothered about the answer.

—Not as bad as what happened to Ant Li, he said, with a puffy-lip grin.

—He hit you?

—Not at first. His mates did. He just joined in after.

—What'd he hit you for?

—Since when'd he need a reason?

He held up his hand. The green-&-silver flashed. Silence.

I pulled my feet out of the pool: MT looked like he was going to join me & I didn't fancy the mingle. Ripples in the soft moonlight—only one moon—a gray glow over the Plaza. The cimarron trees looked eerie—otherworldly.

—Got to go, I said. Curfew coming up.

Basically, MT came with me.

Predictable reaction from Mum. I cut her short, saying he's just a guy from school. They kicked him out of his apartment—surely you can sympathize with that?

I took him on a guided tour. That hardly lasted for

more than a nanosecond—this place is so tiny. Apologized too often. Told him the roof pools were still open if he needed to freshen up (& boy did he need to). He went upstairs. Mum turned on me again.

—Look, I said, you don't have to like him.

—I certainly don't, she says.

—He's got nowhere else to go.

—& where's he going to sleep? The floor? You're not doing it with him in my house.

God—Mum can be so crude. I told her he cd have Lil Sis's room—until SHE kicked up a fuss. She's too young to be neighborly & I guess I don't set her the best example ever. OK OK, so I said he cd have my room. He said he'd sleep on the floor if we had a spare duvet. He actually said he'd sleep in the pool since it's so nice to swim under the stars. I thought of him half naked and splayed out in the water.

—Just have my bedroom, I said.

So here I am writing by the light of Lil Sis's cartoon novelty lamp. She snuffles in her sleep. Actually, I don't know how she can sleep with so many toy animals in the bed. Her room's decorated with dolphins & whales & other alien sea life. Quite soothing, I suppose. I'm too tired to write any more. There's no window. Good. I don't want to see what's going on in the world outside.

22.10

It was bizarre seeing MT for breakfast. He looked grubby still—all prickly & rough.

—Don't you have any clean clothes? I asked.

I got a good glare from Mum for that. She seems to have come around to MT's presence in the place. It probably makes her feel a bit like Big Bro has come home. (God, I wish he wd write! Is he OK?) Lil Sis just got on with her waffles as if nothing else in the world mattered.

—Actually I don't have any more clothes, MT said, going pink around the gills.

I suppose some people wd say the way he tugged at his sweater was quite endearing. Mum ordered me into my room to sort him some things out. I must've looked as outraged as I felt, bcs MT came over all stammery. I told him to sit down & eat. Mum's waffles are offworld. (Every mum shd be good at something.) I cd tell that MT was admiring my stuff—his own clothes look like they come from the bottom of a donation bin. At least he didn't say anything mouthy. He just ruffled his hair up & muttered something like, thank god for unisex. He took my blue sarong—the one Big Bro always used to nick, with the lotus flowers around the bottom. His feet were too big to borrow more reputable sandals. He said thanks for everything but I cd see he didn't want to take it.

Toni V stopped reading in disgust. Who did this Marek T think he was, going into a girl's apartment and nabbing her stuff? And getting into a fight with those A boys! So violent. Marek T sounded like an A1 loser. He wouldn't last five minutes with a drill and slab of concrete. Fuming, Toni V took himself off to the workers' gymnasium to pummel a punch bag. The gym had been set up in a long loft space in a nearby block. It overlooked one of the new building projects.

From the chest-press machine he cast a professional eye over the foundations in the plot outside. Good stuff. Nice alignment. He hadn't seen the plans, but it looked like most of the new buildings in City One—

tall, graceful, and functional, with good-sized pools in the basement, and penthouse flats for execs who liked their own deluxe swimming facilities. Chances were, the individual apartments would be sold already, site unseen. Now that the war was over, City Five was the place to be. The government had finally got around to liberating some money to rebuild it. War damage would soon be a thing of the past—*City Five Alive* and all that. The water quality was good, the people were pretty relaxed and friendly. Toni V had seen a tourism brochure praising the picturesque canal network, and the historic Colonial Museum, complete with a piece of the original coastline arrival pad. (Were those really scorch marks from landing gear? The tourists speculated. It was hard to tell from the photographs.) Toni V hadn't actually been to the museum. It was all stuff from the past, and he knew perfectly well that looking back to the past was a waste of time. Instead, everyone ought to work hard to get *Back to Normal.* Besides, these days he had quite enough problems getting things straight in his head—trying to untangle thoughts about work, the war, and Pelly D. No, he left museums to the brainy types who had nothing better to do.

He had work to be getting on with. *Back to Work! Back to Normal!*

Only work wasn't as satisfying as it used to be, and normal had been looking a bit odd since he'd found the diary of Pelly D.

Stuck with that thought, he got back to clambering across rubble, playing with the fantasy that Marek T had accidentally tripped and fallen into the path of the stone drill. He was a bit ashamed of his bad mood as he pulverized the last remains of the old plaza. Nothing seemed to feel right these days. Even going to Waterworld that time hadn't been as good as he'd hoped.

It was a fantastic place of course—built in the golden age of aquatic decadence, all whitewashed walls and arches hung with gaudy flowers. The centerpiece was a giant water-flume tower, reached by three spiral staircases. The flumes were transparent pipes that wound all around the complex, giving a wet and high-speed view of the cafés, bars, restaurants, and dealers. No expense spared anywhere. Toni V's crowd could just about afford one drink each at the most subdued bar. It wasn't really designed for your basic rough-and-ready type. Toni V felt twitchy on his authentic wood bar stool. He found the drink sickly-sweet, and he was sure the barista was sneering at his callused hands and sun-creased eyes. He watched the girls—all well-groomed with lacquered nails, braided hair, and perfect smiles. It was funny to think of Pelly D parading around with her "offworld" bikini and her gruesome cronies. It was funny to wonder if she hid her hand when she bought a drink.

For a moment Toni V boiled at the unfairness of it all. Then he remembered the Rules and Regulations and that took his temper down a few degrees. You knew where you were with the Rules and Regs. The Rules might be a bit restrictive at times, but at least they didn't change, even if everything outside was being rubbled, then rebuilt. The Rules took away doubt and anxiety. If he'd just followed the Rules, he'd never have been snarled up reading the diary in the first place. Unfortunately, once he'd started reading he'd come across too much stuff that the Rules couldn't help with.

It was like digging up the plaza: you started with a smooth sculptured surface and drilled it until you were standing in a broken landscape where any wrong step could have you tripping and falling.

Too late to go back now. He was already more than halfway through the diary. The only thing he could do was rebuild his opinions and plaster over the uncertainties. Listening to the General would help—maybe he could catch an extra bulletin on the big screen later. The General knew what he was talking about. He was the voice of reason and reassurance. The General said that prejudice was a bad thing, whoever it was against. There was no room for prejudice and envy in the reconstruction of a better life.

There was only hard work and good living—getting things *Back to Normal.*

Going into the pools at Waterworld should've been a major pleasure. Physically it was outstanding—it was pure stuff, one hundred percent filtered—just Bliss to dive into, deep down, for the first time in months, grazing the bottom of the pools with the late sun high above. Everything was quiet underwater—no raucous guys, no drilling, no incessant insect buzzing. No dust, no glare, just the water—cool and divine. So that felt good, mostly. It was coming up to the surface that made him awkward again—fish out of water.

Straightaway he was dunked by Monsumi Q. They fought underwater for a bit and came up half laughing—half spluttering. Mistake. Apparently it was not the sort of rough behavior regular clientele would tolerate. A pool steward hailed them while a group of girls in bikinis stood and watched, like the guys were some kind of zoo exhibit.

Toni V was pretty hacked off about the whole affair, which was unusual for him. Maybe some of Pelly D's uppity ways were rubbing off, he thought. He vented to Monsumi Q: "Coming down on us like that just because we're different! Don't they realize it's guys like us that built this whole damned place?"

Mon Q looked puzzled, as if he'd not thought about it before. "I guess they don't mean it personally."

"Isn't that worse? It's like they're prejudiced against anyone who doesn't come from the top families. Well, they can stuff their fancy pool—I wouldn't want to pollute it for all the pretty princesses!"

Toni V swam away from the rest of the guys, who were horsing around at a game of waterball. He heaved himself up on the edge of the pool and sat there until the sun dimmed completely and the stars prickled out. He felt dizzy—the water was obviously O_2 enriched—giving everyone a high. Most of his anger dripped away and he relaxed. It wasn't so bad. He shouldn't get jumpy just because some low-life pool attendant got rude. He should just let the O_2 do its work.

After a while it did. He smiled. Maybe that was why no one felt bad about the astronomical entrance charge to Waterworld—they were too happy to care. He didn't quite feel as if he deserved it.

That's stupid, he snapped in his head. Of course he deserved it. Builders were every bit as important to the cities as rich dealers. The General himself said so.

City Five was due for a major facelift and he was part of the whole process. It would look lovely when all the new avenues were in place and when the plaza was finished, hopefully in time for the General's long-anticipated visit and the unveiling of the new sculptures. Toni V had asked the Supervisor if he could see the plans for the final renovations. Flattered, the Supervisor had agreed. It had been the midmorning water break after all. Toni V had gulped down his drink and dunked his head quickly under the makeshift shower they'd set up not far from the cimarron grove. The supe pulled the laptop around, out of the glare. Not many people were interested in 3-D projections and subterranean stratification charts. It was a whole new world to Toni V. He'd had to learn everything on-site, from drilling and hauling, to building and reinforcing.

"It's going to be beautiful, isn't it?" the supe said.

Yes. Absolutely yes, it was going to be beautiful. The smooth stretches of old-style concrete and wild flowerbeds were being pulled up to make way for walkways of marble—real high-quality replica stuff. Slow-flowing waterways would run in geometric patterns, and there would be statues of glorious leaders—the heroes who had won the war—set to advantage in a ring of gilt columns. "Wow," he said. "This beats even the Plaza Mayor in City One."

The supe beamed. "Long overdue," he said. "There's a strong feeling that this city has a lot to celebrate. *City Five Alive* and all that."

"Yeah."

"The party piece is going to be a bank of illuminations for the new plaza sign. The best laser-light technology money can buy. No expense spared." He gestured over to the north side of the plaza where the blocks were currently being renovated. They were hidden under giant tarpaulins that hung limp in the heat.

Toni V saw the vision. It would be worth all the dust and the noise and the hard graft. It truly would be beautiful.

The Supervisor remembered who he was talking to. "Back to work, boy-o. Shirking's for—"

"Losers. I know." Toni V grinned. He could tell there were no hard feelings: the ice had been broken. *Onward and upward!*

Looking at the plans had put a few ideas into his head. Mistake? Maybe. Workers like him didn't need ideas. Big muscles and endurance were the essentials; brains were just the icing. But what if he got some training? What if he did some courses and got some proper learning to make up for missing years at school? Then he'd be able to help make the plans as well as help build them. *Onward and upward*, he thought.

Stupid idea, he thought next. As if I'll get ahead doing that. I can't even read properly, let alone do all the computer programming.

He was getting better at reading, though. He was turning the pages of Pelly D's diary more quickly than before.

Halfway back to the drill, a storm of noise started up. Two big digging machines had rumbled their way through the quiet avenues and now they were gorging on the land that Toni V's crew had broken up. Giant mechanical jaws reached down and gulped up chunks of concrete. Most of the Demo Crew had stopped to watch the machines at work.

"A week's worth of power ration in every minute's work," complained one of the guys. It was true. Humans could have done the job much more cheaply. Still, it was awesome to watch them, pulling up the old stuff to make way for the new.

Then Toni V's heart flipped over with anxiety. He only saw it for a moment—a bundle of white papers in a clear plastic folder. A second later the papers were swallowed up in the machine's giant maw: mangled and ruined with rock and earth and concrete—all set for the landfill.

No one else took the blindest bit of notice of the papers. Toni V tried not to. He focused on his drilling, telling himself that even if it had been another diary, that was hardly of world-shattering importance. It would just be someone's random life, like Pelly D's random emotions. Only an idiot would bury a diary in a public place where anyone could come along and find it, anyway. A normal, rational person would keep a diary safely in an apartment, at the very least hidden somewhere simple, like behind a loose tile in the bathroom wall.

There was a muted thump from the east side of the city as another abandoned block was brought to the ground. Toni V wondered what the noise of bombs had sounded like. He couldn't remember. Then he wondered if people had chosen to bury things in the plaza because it hadn't been a target for bombing like the apartment blocks. They'd have buried their things planning to come back after the War to find them . . . to start their cushy lives over again in a nicer part of town. No doubt that was exactly what Pelly D meant to do. Or perhaps she'd moved on and no longer cared about looking for her diary. For one blood-racing moment Toni V thought, what if Pelly D had been killed in a bomb explosion?

Crazy idea!

People like Pelly D were just too full of life for that. Besides, if she'd died she wouldn't have finished her diary and she wouldn't have come out onto the plaza to bury it, would she?

Which might still mean she'd be back looking for it.

He had to laugh at himself: there he was, lifting his goggles and looking around suddenly as if Pelly D was about to appear from behind a cimarron saying, "Coo-ee, anyone seen my diary?"

Wouldn't she have better things to do?

"I have better things to do," he muttered, and another section of plaza was reduced to rubble. Well, hadn't the diary said: *Dig—dig everywhere*?

At the end of the shift word got around quickly about the accident. Everyone was stunned. The medic doled out quick-fix pep pills and prepared the morgue: golden boy Hoodie N had died when a wall on Hanger Lane collapsed on him and his crew. Five other guys were killed, Kiw P among them.

23.10

Exams. Hate 'em.

The following E-day, Toni V was pulled from the plaza. His name came up on the big screen during breakfast. He was to be part of a detail of fifty workers leaving for Hanger Lane. Everyone knew what that was all about. Salvage Squad!

"Grim pickings," said Credula N.

"They are not!" objected one of the new recruits—the one who was still freaked at being away from home. "There aren't any bodies. That's just bull."

Cred N smiled wolfishly. "I heard there were skellingtons and everything."

"Are not!"

"Are too!"

"Quit the kids' talk," Toni V grouched. "Let's just be glad the war's over."

Because they were off to a bomb site.

Hood N was stiff in the morgue, set out neat in a row with the others and only the medic to watch over. There was no chance to ask if he'd rigged the transfer, though he probably had. It was funny to think that Hood N was influencing things, even though he himself was cold and dead. It was funny to think that someone like Hood N *could* be dead. Toni V kept expecting him to come bursting into view with his usual health and energy. Several times he'd looked up from work, thinking he'd seen Hoodie some way off, walking across the plaza. Once, he thought he heard Hood N shouting outside the block. When he looked over, he saw it was only a bunch of the Demo Crew, laughing in the late-afternoon sunlight.

And yes, even though Hood N was dead, the sun kept shining as if nothing had changed. Toni V hoped that the Salvage Squad got good water rations; it was going to be another achingly hot day.

The new Supervisor was a solid chunk of woman with muscles on her muscles. She called the fresh batch of workers over for a briefing. "My name's Wim Vellora and I'm as lovely as I look." No one dared laugh. Her face was as dry as old leather, her hair was a violent shade of scarlet and her eyes were blank.

"Now the first squad've been in to look around. They say it's sound—no live ammo, at any rate. We hope." She held up white flashcards showing images of small round metal devices. "These are the key land mines that might still be inside. This one in particular is a funeral waiting to happen. Do not go near the buggers if this red lever's no longer attached. I'm serious, guys—hands off, or hands off, if you know what I mean. And more than *hands*: fella over down by the canal thought he'd do the hero thing with one of these babies, and let's just say he won't be passing his genes on for the next generation." The young men all winced. Just as she meant them to. Wim Vellora continued. "If you see anything tottering, *run for it*, no heroics. You all heard what happened to my sweet boy Hoodie last week." She waited long enough for this to sink in. "And last thing—it ain't true what you hear: there's no old bodies or bones from the War. The San took care of 'em, what was left of 'em. We hope. The Demo Crew's job is to haul this sorry crap out into the skips. You've all seen the narrow avenues around this block—no hope of anything mechanical till we've blasted our way clear. Before they do that we want to make sure there's nothing valuable left inside—get it? We're talking plastics and metals that can be recycled, intact electrics—all that stuff. Don't even think about pilfering stuff, guys. I'll be conducting spot searches personally, and don't go supposing that groping your sweaty bodies gives me even a nanothrill. It doesn't. You know the Rules and Regs—hefty punishments for anyone caught looting *anything*. And, hey, the punishments I dole out might just give me more than a nanothrill.

"Now—this is grunt work today, boys. Hard hats at all times and water breaks when you hear the siren.

Questions? Nope? Good—cos I ain't got answers for you. Now move it!"

It was still hard work, even if he wasn't wrestling with a drill with a mind of its own. The gang fanned out over the block and began trawling through the nearest trash. Someone had helpfully propped up the most precarious walls. Toni V couldn't look at them without thinking of Hood N and his big flash of a smile.

The building Toni V was allocated to had obviously suffered collateral damage from a bomb, but no direct hit. The entire front of the block had sagged, leaving a view of the rooms inside. Although many of the floors had collapsed, some were intact. Some still had smashed TV screens on the walls, or smudged pictures. Some still had blasted furniture.

Toni V set to work sorting the debris. He tried to switch off his mind—not think about the people who'd once lived and worked in the buildings. It wasn't so bad at first. With his new workmate—a weedy guy called Appel F—he shifted half-melted plastic doors, rubble, glass, everything. Then he started to notice the little bits and pieces. They were all a uniform dust color, but there was no mistaking the shapes. Forks, books, boots. The forks were bent, the books were burnt, and the boots were mismatched. Toni V hauled them all out. All the things that made up an ordinary life, things that had survived long after their owners were gone. The salvage Dumpsters were filling quickly.

31.10

It's not really War. People keep calling it that, but they're just being retro. They're thinking of Earth & the pre-Colony stuff. That's not what this planet's about. There's never been a War, so why shd we have one now? It's just a word. That doesn't make it a thing that's happening—happening in three Cities out of five. So there are bombs? So there are missiles? It's political violence; it's mechanical aggression, it's downright rude, but it doesn't have to be War. Y Bretton said Civil War tore Earth apart.

Point being? DON'T DO IT, GUYS!

End result: three people dead in the latest explosion.

They're unreeling spiky wire fences across the Plaza & down some of the avenues. I hope they don't think anyone's going to have dramatic Last Stands under my grove of cimarron! Thank god it'll never get that far. Overseas, the O-HA have really woken up now. They're sending in a peacekeeping task force & those grunts mean Business. General Saint-Antel said that the O-HA formally responded to our plea for help at first dawn this morning. He's back in my good books again cos it takes a lot to ask for help when everyone else in the City Government thinks you're overreacting. I'd like to know what cd be overreacting, when you've got Atsumisi bully-boys camping outside the City & Atsumisi bully-boys running the joint from the inside.

Mum is sure we can hold out long enough for the O-HA to get here from Overseas. Wonder if they'll send troops on the Marie-Cloud—I haven't seen her for ages. It's good to know they're coming & that the War'll be over soon, then we can all get on with picking up the pieces and saying sorry guys, didn't mean to blow your house up; my mistake, mate.

Dad's business has temporarily relocated him to City One, where there isn't any danger from the bombs. He says he's put in an order to have us transferred with him, but that cd take weeks to process, given the hairy situation here. The words "rat," "ship," and "sinking" come to mind. I feel entirely betrayed by my father, my City, & the whole damn Colony.

If only they'd drop a Big One on school. (Sooner, rather than later, so I can quit trying to revise while the explosions are going off like supernovae.)

Toni V didn't want to read about the war. Working day after day in the aftermath, he was just glad that it was all over. *Back to Normal,* the General said. Toni V repeated the words over and over. Recently they'd been sounding a bit hollow. What was "normal"? Could they go back to how things had been before the war? No matter how many new buildings went up and how many new lives were grown, you couldn't really undo damage, could you? He was starting to understand that no matter how determined or ambitious Pelly D was, her life after the war could never be the same again.

Unconsciously, he scratched the ID on the back of his hand as he worried. He was hunched over on the top bunk and turned the diary to catch second-moon light from the window. He skimmed through a lot of entries. It was no fun reading about rationing and job restrictions—but more fun than thinking about Hood N and Kiw P laid out side by side in the cold room with only the medic to keep them company.

35.10

The City's calm. People are out on the streets smiling again. There's talk, of course, always talk about the Galrezi stirring up trouble. They say if it wasn't for us, there wdn't be fighting & bombing. They say we're not neighborly. That's fine, considering how many people refuse to be "neighborly" enough to sit next to a G at school. Most of the Atsumisi are acting superior. I know for a fact that some of Dad's business colleagues have "temporarily" moved into our apartment. How nice for them. They sent word that we could come over & pick up some more of our stuff (only because they want to make room for their own stuff). It was awful having to go back home, just me & Mum, & seeing all our things there as if nothing had happened—all the pictures on the wall & the books on the shelf, & Dad's pair of hiking boots still muddy & abandoned in the utility room. I guess it's going to be a while before we all go off on one of those god-awful family rambles again. We always said we'd take another hike past the East Canal & see the sawri bird colonies there. Right up to today I would have just keeled over & died at the mere thought. Now it seems kind of sweet, all of us going out in the sun. Maybe I'll suggest we do it when Big Bro gets back, when this stink of a mess is over. Better still, I'll suggest we all go for a sail on the Marie-Cloud.

We took our time, picking out things we wanted. Funny, we didn't go for all the gadgets, things that Dad measures success by. We loaded our bags with personal stuff. & I got some more clothes, of course. A girl can only be seen in the same top so many times.

The Atsumisi in our house gave us a hamper of

luxury food to take with us. I can't believe people can be so two-faced. It's the same at school. Students I used to hang out with all the time, now they cross over to the other side of the corridor with sickly sad grins—you know, how you get if a beggar ever asks for spare change & you say, sorry I haven't got any.

I still don't sit next to Marek T—I don't know if he expects me to. I only walk to school with him bcs it's polite & bcs Hanna S from over the corridor has been sent on the latest ferry going to City One. Bizarre—everything else in this City is going to pieces and the only things still Business As Usual are: (a) school & (b) ships out of here.

I asked MT if he wanted to come to Waterworld one evening—my season ticket is valid for two till the end of summer—but he said no. His loss.

39.10

No new skirmishes for four days now. Security has eased up a little. About time too. It's getting so you can't go down an avenue without someone stopping for a "friendly" little chat. Is it just me, or are most Galrezi starting a new fashion for long sleeves that cover the backs of the hands?

40.10

HOURS of revision later. What's my problem?!! Must be spending too much time around Brainbox No-Life of the Year—yes, the man MT himself. I'll be s-o-o-o glad when all the exams are over. No news from Dad. It's not like Big Bro, who's probably in hiding from the draft somewhere. Dad's just not writing. We know he cd. He's Atsumisi: apparently they can do whatever the hell they like. He sends money regularly, so I'm still getting my allowance. It's not so much fun spending it now. More demos against Galrezi outside City Hall. The anti-anti-Galrezi demo never got off the ground. Not enough people dared turn up. Not surprising. I've seen where they take people.

41.10

Oh god. Maybe I shdn't write this. I have to. There's no one to tell. The gang at school might as well be on another planet. Mum's warped worrying over work & art & Big Bro's still being gone.

The thing is, MT said my name tonight. Wow. So simple. We were sitting up on the roof. Only one moon out. We'd been lolling around in the water. Most people don't swim that late & they can hardly curfew what you do on your own rooftop, can they? So we went up to swim. It was otherworldly, sloshing about in the cool water, just wet shapes in the dark. Then MT sat on the edge of the pool & looked at the stars. He was doing this thing with his fingers—like touching the universe. That's just like Gim D: Big Bro used to lie flat on his back & put his hand up & say: Look Pelly, I can put the starlight out.

I had this sudden picture of Big Bro Overseas playing with the stars. I hope he's OK. Of course he's OK.

Then I remembered the reality of MT getting in the

way of my view. He stroked the universe with his fingertips & said: It doesn't seem so far away, does it?

I stayed in the water for a bit longer. Now we don't have our own pool I like to keep underwater as long as possible.

—No gene tags up there, MT said. Just atoms, or heaven, whichever way you look at it.

I bobbed under the surface for a moment. It's too much, thinking about things like that. About how simple things wd be if they were just . . . simple. When I came up to air again MT was looking straight at me.

—Why don't you ever say my name? he asked.

—I do, I lied.

(Why shd I say his name?!)

—It's like you look straight through me sometimes. Like I'm the stars & you can just block me out with your hand.

—I don't, I lied.

—Look at me then.

So I looked. Had to look away. He's not got all gold chains & body art like Ant Li, but he's so fit & lean. His muscles looked so sleek in the moonlight.

—Pelly, he said.

I can still hear his voice, all raw. When he said my name like that I shivered.

—Pelly Damson, he said. Ever thought what you'll do when you leave school & you're P Damson?

That made me uncomfortable. Sure I want to be older & get to do more or less what I want, but I don't want to be P Damson. I want to be just PELLY. Me. I was going to tell MT about sailing on the Marie-Cloud, but he made some fatuous comment about me becoming a professional shopper so I didn't. He said he was going to join the O-HA & go to work Overseas as soon as he was old enough to have a travel permit.

—& fight the world's evils single-handedly I suppose?

Just before we went inside he said: You hate having me here, don't you? Why'd you invite me?

—Bcs I felt sorry for you! I snapped.

He laughed at that. A sharp laugh. Surprisingly, he didn't throw a fit.

—I don't blame you, he said. Why shdn't you pity me? My life was light-years from yours.

I hated him for saying that. Bcs he used the past tense. My life USED to be better than anyone's. Now our lives are as good as the same. The only difference is that I can remember what it was like to have more. Remember?! It was only last week! Bit by bit they're taking it all away from me & I can't do a damn thing about it. Can't riot, can't vote, can't make it all stop.

—Hey, Pelly, don't cry.

I wasn't! (Much.)

—I know your stupid name, I said, climbing out of the pool & heading straight for my towel.

—Marek Tallin's a loser! I shouted out to the night sky. & Marek didn't seem to mind.

42.10

I think about him—his smooth skin, how his hair looked, wet against his cheek. He shaves more often now (I shd know, I have to wait in line for the washroom).

His face looks good. He's still Marek T, tho. I didn't speak to him over breakfast this morning. He probably never noticed. The TV was on—lots of gumph about General Insidian heading our way for a peace treaty. He'd best be quick. Overseas will be Over Here to sort them out in no time. Does MT still like me? He used to moon over me all the time, but he's gone all prickly now & distant. Typical. I hate him.

I won't be writing much from now on. Exam season is upon us.

3.1

No school, thanks to New Year holidays. Doesn't feel much like a holiday. Who wants to watch the fireworks when we've got sporadic explosions? The usual New Year Matsuri has been cancelled: no one dares join in a public festival, so we had a mini-Matsuri at home: me n Lil Sis made paper lanterns & we burned incense & wrote wishes to our Lucky Star. My wish was all-encompassing: JUST MAKE EVERYTHING ALL RIGHT

AGAIN. Lil Sis asked for a dolphin. I didn't have the heart to tell her they're extinct.

At least I survived two weeks of exams. & now I know I'm not going to die young, bcs, god, if I was I'd arrange it so that it was BEFORE that sort of AGONY. Who invented exams? Why weren't they strangled in the test tube? I bet they were Atsumisi, whoever they were.

Cdn't get my exam results on-line either, cos on-line is permanently off-line, unless you want to log on & get endless pictures of General Insidian smirking. Spam propaganda sucks. I feel awful. Mum says there must be a bug in the water. Marek's feeling iffy too. I call him Marek now. Not to his face of course. He didn't seem to care about the results, even tho he studied a gazillion times harder than anyone else at school.

—What's the point? he says.

—Lots of point, I said. The War's not going to go on forever . . .

Thank god it hadn't, Toni V thought, wondering what it was like to take an exam. Pretty bad by the sound of it.

4.1

Pathetic New Year celebrations are NOTHING compared to this incredible dancing-on-top-of-the-world, into-orbit GOOD NEWS!!! Big Bro got a letter through, yep, a note with his big black signature—Gim Damson!!

An old school friend came by after curfew. Mum didn't want to let him in—there's no end of trouble for anyone crossing the Plaza fence without proper authorization.

Is it safe for you to be here? I asked, thinking of all those draft dodgers swimming for freedom on the night my brother left.

This guy—he didn't tell us his name—just held up his

hand showing his red stamp & he grinned. (Why's he being nice if he's an A? I suppose I'd forgotten that some Atsumisi are OK—in fact, most all of them probably wd be if they weren't being brainwashed by the Heritage Clan & if they didn't get free apartments & cushy jobs for being down on Galrezi. Sorry Dad, but that goes for you too.)

It turns out Big Bro has gone Overseas for sure. Lucky b*****d. He's managed to join up with the O-HA, so he cd even be coming over with one of the official peacekeeping missions! We'll wait n see over the next few months . . . It cracks me up, knowing the O-HA are coming to see if there have been any humanitarian abuses: I cd fill a whole diary with a list of them!

Mum fetched the guy food from downstairs, cos he wdn't eat in the communal kitchen. Not for the usual reasons (it's foul) but bcs he doesn't want to be spotted on CCTV monitors. It doesn't do for the Atsumisi to visit Galrezi unless it's Security business. He asked if Marek had had his draft notification yet. Marek shook his head.

—When it comes, the guy said, don't go. Just don't go.

—I don't want to go, Marek said.

—Whatever you do or don't want to do, don't go. D'you know how many thousands have gone already?

We looked blank. The City Governors have been pretty cagey about that.

—More importantly, said the guy, do you know how many people have come back? I'm not saying anything, bcs I don't know anything. It just makes you wonder, that's all.

(Poor Sassy B! Are they keeping her there? Is she all right?)

The guy wdn't stay the night. I saw him to the door. He ruffled my hair.

—Your big bro sends a special hi to you, Pelly D. Says you got to take care of yourself. Oh & he asked after someone called Moma Peg too.

Well he wd. We've both been hanging out with Moma Peg since we were wee small things. I told the guy about Moma Peg getting taken to the "hospital" ages ago & his face went gray. He didn't comment. He didn't need to. But Big Bro is OK & that's the main thing. We cdn't get a message to Dad—he's not yet back from City One—something about new zoning regulations means that he has to live near his main point of work. Nice to know the A's are messing the A's around too, with all the new Rules & Regulations. There's no way Dad wd be able to come & live with us, even if he wanted to: the block is being cleared of Mazzini & the few Atsumisi who are left. The Big Screen in the hallway has an announcement about it.

The news about Big Bro kind of makes up for today's HUMILIATION. I thought I'd die. I'll definitely sue Waterworld off the face of this planet, as soon as this mess is over. Revoking my pass is just the Final Insult! They just can't treat people like that! They certainly can't treat ME like that!

I feel crappy.

She wrote a bit more about not feeling well. Toni V skipped those bits as often as he could. Pelly D wasn't supposed to be poorly. She was sassy and sexy and full of life. And if she was feeling crappy, well, that had nothing to do with the water. City supplies had never been poisoned during the war—that was just an urban myth started by irresponsible dissidents and finished by the triumph of common sense: the General himself had said so. And if people got upset about water shortages, well it had been happening all over the colony!

Pelly D seemed to take it pretty badly though. Toni V was sorry to read the bit about her getting barred from going to Waterworld, along with all the other Galrezi. It was a shame. Going there would have cheered her up. Still, everyone knew that you had to do what was best for the whole community. You had to follow the Rules and Regulations—everyone making sacrifices for the greater good and all that. Some people had privileges and some didn't—that's the way a healthy society worked. It was obvious. Even Toni V could understand that much.

It was funny to think of people being banned from places. Toni V vaguely remembered the old pre-war propaganda. He'd seen peeling relics of the old A & M Only signs. When the signs faded after the war they weren't replaced; they just weren't needed anymore. People just didn't go shoving their way in where they weren't wanted any longer; they naturally fell into their proper spheres. Wasn't that why he was on the Salvage Squad, and not doing megadeals in some offworld office? You had to know your job and get on with it.

As for discrimination, that was old news. It didn't fit the new image—all the posters around town, under the *City Five Alive* slogan. The ads showed happy, healthy families wallowing in luxury pools together, surrounded by posh new buildings and brand-new parks. That was what they were working for, the General said.

Toni V slept uneasily that night. Now that he'd switched work his ears were no longer ringing from the drill, and the silence unnerved him. That day on the salvage site, the sounds had all been strange and dulled—a sudden rush of rubble as he put a foot wrong; a flow of dust when he disturbed anything; the muted sound of men working elsewhere in the building; the crash as debris was hauled out and flung into a Dumpster.

He'd found a buried book toward the end of the mid-afternoon shift. He'd hoped it would be a diary but it was just a novel. He flipped through the pages. The print was tiny and it didn't look all that interesting. Would there be another diary? There were mangled laptops, yes, but no diary. Where had all the diaries gone? Where had all the people gone who buried the diaries? Why was he looking for diaries anyway, when he was supposed to be keeping an eye out for important stuff to salvage . . . and for tottering walls? Toni V had thrown the novel in the Dumpster, just as he was supposed to.

His mind shifted from memory into restless sleep.

In his dreams he was digging. He was digging in a frenzy. He was digging with the crazy idea that all the people he'd ever known were buried underground—under the great plaza in City Five. He'd drilled away the concrete slabs and he was digging through the dusty earth with his shovel. He kept finding packages of letters, diaries, and photographs, but every time he reached into the hole the pages would crumble and the pictures would disappear. Then he dreamed he was trying to find his own diary—a diary he'd never written, with page after page about his life. He knew something bad would happen if he didn't find it so he kept on digging. The hole got deeper and deeper. The farther he stretched the harder it was to reach. He didn't want to fall in the hole. He tried to climb out, but sand started pouring in, till he was up to his gills in it and panicking. There was no air—no moisture—he couldn't breathe—couldn't wake up.

19.1

Three weeks into the New Year & there's STILL not enough water. We're reduced to carry-along water cans. It's so humiliating, standing in line at the emergency standpipes. Everyone wants more water than they're allowed. The rationing is disgraceful—there's no need for it. We had plenty of water before summer. The reservoirs are full & it'll soon be getting cooler. They haven't even predicted a dry winter. So why aren't we allowed fresh bathing water? People have started siphoning water from the rooftop pools. Now we have to have a kind of sentry posted up there to make sure that people in the apartment block use the water fairly. Everyone looks awful—dry & flaky. Lil Sis was crying & fretting most of today. I keep rubbing moisturizer cream on her face & neck. She says she wants to go to Waterworld with her friends. Nothing you can say to that. I want the same. I have to make do with standing on the roof and looking out over the City. It still looks beautiful from high up, part-proud, part-crumbled, like a half-eaten cake. Dust rises from the bomb sites & there's smoke near the East Canal. Not very environmentally friendly. Apparently no one's worried about that anymore.

We all just want water.

21.1

Water ration doubled. Ironic. Nobody's happy—the only reason there's more water is bcs more families have had their orders to go & work in other Cities. The Atsumisi are letting them thru the barricades of course. It's a funny War. It's still City Five, but it's not like our City any longer. They're doing hand scans at the edge of the

Plaza, supposedly to make sure that rebellious Galrezi aren't lurking about waiting to blow up the A's. Nobody knows what's going on. Is General Saint-Antel really going to make peace with Insidian? And if he is, can we get it over & done quickly so things can come back to NORMAL? I can't believe I'm writing this, but I just want to get back to school & find out my exam results.

22.1

School canceled.

I'm sitting at the table looking at my old textbooks. Marek's already thrown his out of the window. His draft notice was posted on the Big Screen in the hall downstairs. Nobody "officially" knows where he is. Will they go trawling thru old CCTV recordings to spot him? Maybe he'll be safe until Overseas get here to end the War & sort everything out. There are cameras all over the City. You cdn't hide for long if you really had to. Moma Peg always said that if your heart was pure you'd never have reason to hide. Bet she'd change her tune if she cd see us now. Maybe she can. I know what happens in those "hospitals" now: Moma Peg truly cd be atoms in the atmosphere—wafting over the City or just blowing around this damned planet Home From Home. Can she see the Overseas troops? Are they nearly here yet?

Whole areas of the City need complete rebuilding.

I need a swim.

25.1

I'm on water duty all the time now. Mum is too ill to go down & obviously Marek can't go out. I hear him pacing up & down in my old bedroom. On the other side of the barbed wire the City is business as usual. I suppose on this side we're too far away for people to see how rough we look. Probably just as well. I don't want anyone to see how shabby I am. (Mum gave away half our moisturizer cream. Some people down the hall didn't have any at all. They'd been dipping their gills in the drinking-water ration, but they'd gone all scabby & cracked. Gross. I think I'll jump out of the window before I get that bad.) We're praying for rain.

31.1

The days are going past so quickly, but each one seems endless at the time. If I didn't have this diary I don't think I'd even know what day it is. We don't do much. We're afraid now. Mum tries to keep us jolly by suggesting silly pen-&-paper games that she used to play when she was a kid. Only paper's rationed.

—Don't you have a diary, Pelly D? she asked. We cd have a few pages out of that.

—No!! I said.

Marek looked at me funny.

—You keep a diary? he asked.

—Believe it or not, I can write.

—Don't take offense, he said. I was thinking of writing a diary myself, so that when this is all over we'll have a record of it.

I didn't bother arguing with him. It's not as if I

MEANT this diary to be a record of anything ludicrously grim! I almost hate the wretched thing for existing—for being proof that my golden life turned to crap. Yes, crap. The only thing that keeps me going & keeps me writing this is the thought that the War will soon be over. General Saint-Antel will see us through, & the O-HA troops from Overseas shd be here soon. (Cd my Big Bad Bro be with them?! No more news, but we are hopeful.) Maybe then we'll be able to get in touch with Dad again. Mum says he's probably tried to get hold of us, but they're not even letting Atsumisi cross the Plaza anymore & the only electronic info we get is on the Big Screen downstairs. The power's often cut off for most of the day.

I haven't been shopping for three weeks. Or, put another way, three weeks ago I was still going shopping. I think it's the little things you miss—like nipping out for an ice cream, or a drink at the Milky Way. Or just going for an offworld haircut.

32.1

Marek asked if he cd read my diary. NO WAY!! Then he had the nerve to ask if he was mentioned in it. Doesn't he think I have better things to write about?

—When the War's over you can publish your diary & give keynote speeches at O-HA dinners & things, he said. You'll be a famous author.

—I don't want to publish anything, I said. It's not about anything except my life.

Yeah, my fabulous life. I'd trade in all my gorgeous clothes for a deep puddle to sit in right now. There's a rumor going around that the Atsumisi are deliberately stopping or contaminating water supplies to Galrezi blocks. Wd they really do that? It can't be deliberate. Don't they know what'll happen if we don't get more water soon? If they want us to go off & build their special irrigation system they'd be better off glutting us up on water so we're fit & happy. And why aren't they getting Galrezi workers off the City One draft list to work on OUR water problem? That's what I want to know.

34.1

Cdn't sleep last night—too hot & dry. Lil Sis was wheezing badly, so I got up to fix a drink—we've still got box juices & bottles of Blue Mountain, thank goodness. Bumped into Marek in the living room. He was standing at the window with his forehead pressed to the plastic. There was a bit of paper in his hand. (Yeah, the hard-copy mail still gets thru, but only when it's bad news.) Before I asked what the paper was, I knew. It was a printout of draft names. With mine on it. Pelly Damson. My full name. Not me, though. They cdn't be asking for me. I'm Pelly D, not a conscript worker! I'm Pelly D, not a Galrezi gene tag! I crumpled the paper up.

—I didn't want to show your mum, he said.

—Thanks. She's worried enough as it is.

—She's not taking her full water ration, you know.

I knew. She was giving lots of it to Lil Sis. So were me n Marek. Stupid really, making ourselves so weak we wdn't be able to look after her. But Lil Sis is too little to understand that it's not for much longer now. We hacked into a pirate news site that said the O-HA Peacekeepers have landed & are marching to City Four. Will they liberate it? Will they side with Insidian? I'm hopeful. General Saint-Antel is trying to find a way to join forces with them. The City Five Governors are holed up in a "neutral zone" in the northeast of the City, not far from the East Canal. They'll soon go into action, though. (Hope they don't trash the prairie land around the Canal. We used to go there on school trips, to film sawri birds & collect wildflowers. I remember Sassy B was allergic to this tall grass they have there & she broke out in a rash all over her legs. MT gave her some skin cream. He was always doing geeky helpful things like that.)

Funny—one of the places that got blown up last night was our school, we saw it on the Big Screen. I thought I'd be over the moon to see it black & smoking. I wasn't. Fifty-four dead, two hundred and seventeen wounded. Yeah—all Atsumisi & Mazzini ironically. It was a big mistake. They fired the missile in good faith at some other "dissident" target—then claimed the school was just "collateral damage." Bcs no G's were hurt, General Insidian is saying that the G's did it themselves as propaganda to get sympathy from Overseas. That's so dumb! G's don't even have an army, let alone proper weapons, apart from homemade bombs. I wish we did have weapons, then we cd fight back ourselves, instead of relying on the Governors to do everything. At least I didn't die at school. Apparently Galrezi don't need an education, hence no school. We're to be workers for the Greater Good. I'm sick of that expression—Greater Good. What's so Great or Good about anything these days? They're taking everything away from us bit by bit. Soon there'll only be one thing left. They wdn't take that, wd they?

—We've just got to hold out for the O-HA coming from Overseas, I said to Marek. I touched his arm, he looked so lost. He shook his head.

—The O-HA won't be able to do much against Insidian, he said. They might not even want to, since they get so much money from the A's. You know, they'll clear this block soon. We'll all have to go. Even your mum and sis.

—Where can we go? If everywhere's as bad as this, where can they send us where there'll be enough water?

—That's just it, Pelly, he said. It's not about water. It never was, & there isn't anywhere to send us. Nowhere we'll walk out of in a hurry. If things go on like this . . .

—Don't!

I guess what he means. I just can't think about it yet. We've all stopped mentioning the people who've gone & who've never come back. We don't think about the big fires that blow smoke over the City. There'll be a perfectly reasonable explanation for it all once the O-HA are here & General Saint-Antel can get the City straight again.

—Oh, you're just tired & thirsty, I said to Marek. My head's killing me too, practically all the time now.

He seemed to pull himself together.

—You're right. Sorry to be gloomy, Pelly.

& that's when it happened. The kissing thing. He sort

of looked down at me in the twin moonlight & then moved closer, & before I knew it his lips were brushing mine—really shy at first, like he'd not kissed a girl in eons, or like he'd wanted to kiss one in particular & cdn't quite believe he finally had. I kissed him back. I might as well write it; no one's ever going to read this diary now.

I was shy too at first. We just kept brushing lips & nibbling lips. Then we kissed properly & that was better than drowning—his body so close to mine & mine just melting into his. I think we just about kissed forever.

Then we heard Mum coughing in the bedroom. We snuck out onto the roof & kissed up there. We didn't even look at the flares of fire away off in the distance; we didn't hear the crackle of weapons somewhere out west. We just kissed endlessly. I tasted every bit of his skin on his face & his neck. His eyes were closed. That looked divine in the moonlight. His throat was arched back. I kissed that too & the soft warmth of his chest.

I know what happened next. He knows too. We only stopped when the rain came. Can you believe the rain came?! I've never been naked in the rain before, at least, not since I was a kid. Our skins just drank it up. Big fat drops fell into the murky puddles at the bottoms of the pools. We had to scramble for our clothes as people came up from the apartments to dance about in the sky-full of water. Soon Marek's face was a sheen of water & smile. I hope I looked as happy. I felt it. Mum found us sometime after. I picked up Lil Sis & swung her around in the water. She laughed & laughed as she was spinning around. I was v conscious of Marek being there. We all ran downstairs to get whatever containers we cd find. Everyone else did the same—the roof was such a jumble! Every-sized water can there is, with raindrops plinking into the bottom. We stretched out plastic sheeting to collect the runoff. Then, when the clouds finally pulled away some time before first dawn, we had to carry all those sloshing cans of water back downstairs again. Still smiling.

& now I'm in my bedroom. Mum didn't say anything when I followed Marek in there. She was carrying Lil Sis, whose curls were all plastered flat to her forehead, & whose thumb was very contentedly in her mouth.

All dreamy still. I'm writing quietly. I don't want to wake him. I was lying with him, all curled up in his arms, but even tho my body was sleeping, my mind wdn't. I was thinking about this diary. Thinking about what he said, about having a record. It doesn't seem right only to write the rough stuff that's been happening. Now I know for sure in my heart that everything's going to be OK, I want to record how HAPPY I am tonight. Big Bro will be nearer soon & when he comes we'll have a big banner out: "WELCOME HOME, GIM DAMSON!" We'll put all this stupid stuff behind us & start working out a way to live together properly again, like we did before all this crap started. I'll go back to school & get my exams sorted. I'll still work on the Marie-Cloud. I might be able to persuade Marek to come with me. He looks lovely asleep—so young & boyish, but dignified too. Why didn't I notice it before?

53.1

I'm afraid. They're clearing the block. We can pack one bag & we have to leave everything else. It's been two days since they stopped bothering with draft orders. There was an emergency meeting down in the basement. Marek & I stood at the back. I was in his arms with his breath on my neck. There's a plan to resist. Everyone's calling it "human export." Worse than that, Marek heard from a guy who heard from a woman—a Mazzini laborer on the canals—that it's true: people aren't always being sent to proper work programs. We don't know what to do. But we'll do whatever we have to. I think we can make it.

Marek isn't so sure. After the meeting we went up to the roof & sat on the edge of the empty pool dangling our legs. Whatever happens, we'll all stick together. Knowing that makes my heart a fraction lighter. I held his hand. Tightly.

—Where are they going to take us? I asked.

He kissed my eyes.

—Will we come back?

He kissed my lips.

Toni V turned the page and swore so vehemently that Monsumi Q woke up on the bunk below.

"You having nightmares or something?"

"Something," Toni V grouched. The moonlight was dipping low—but it was still strong enough for him to see that he'd been cheated. The diary stopped right there, on the evening of the fifty-third. After that, blank pages.

Now he wanted to know what happened next—he wanted to know that everything was going to be all right for Pelly D. What was the point of her keeping a diary if she didn't write what happened in it? It was that Marek T's fault—distracting her. Great.

He flipped back through the diary, touching the

pages. As he reread sections and sentences Pelly D's life leaped out at him and was vivid once more.

He turned over, making the bunk rock.

"You sure you're okay?" Monsumi Q hoisted himself upright on the bunk below. Toni V hid Pelly D's book—not quickly enough. "What you got there?"

"Nothing."

"Pretty solid-looking square of nothing," said Mon Q.

"Nothing that matters." Toni V was doubly sick by then. Monsumi Q knew the Rules and Regs as well as anybody. He might report him . . . might get a reward for seeing that he got his just punishments for meddling in things that were none of his business.

Monsumi Q yawned. "I used to read a lot," he said. "Before I got the draft here."

That was a surprising confession. Looking at Mon Q's broad shoulders and rough hands, Toni V had assumed that he was just a laborer like himself. "Don't you read now?"

"Sure, when I get a chance. I had a library membership

at the last job. Yeah, I used to read a hell of a lot. A book a week sometimes."

"Supreme."

"So what are you reading? Anything good?"

"No! Nothing good. Just a work manual."

The fear started up again. It was one thing to read, quite another to be caught with . . . with this.

Toni V drifted off eventually. Sleep was broken and dry again. He got up before the alarm siren to go to the pool while it was still empty. The water cleared his head and settled his temper a bit.

It was just a diary after all. It was just a thing he'd found in the ground while digging. He very nearly hadn't. He could easily have thrown it away in the water can and then he'd never have had to deal with all these thoughts and feelings. Well, now the diary was finished. He was done with it. It wasn't important. He never knew the girl. It was just one girl. What was the point of hanging on to it? It would only get him into trouble—serious trouble. It could blow all his plans to study more, maybe apprentice to the Supervisor.

"Besides, I'm just one guy in one city. What difference can I make, even if I have read this diary?" The thought seemed so clear when underwater.

Onward and upward.

Slowly his head rose above the water and he opened his mouth to breathe with lungs again. He told himself that he felt much better. He passed the medic on the way to breakfast and manufactured a Pelly D–confident sort of grin.

The medic looked at him curiously and shrugged. He knew from long experience that excess exposure to the sun did funny things to the workers. Too bad it was getting to Toni V. He quite liked the boy; thought he was a quiet, decent sort who could be counted on to slog away rebuilding a city he could never afford to live in. With a sigh, the medic continued on his way back to the sanatorium, scuffing his sandals on the peeling plastic floor. The broken bodies in the morgue were due for release. Their cremation fires would be more heat on an already sweltering day.

Toni V decided to take the diary with him to the

bomb site that day. There was no room for being sentimental. He had work to do. There were Rules. It would be much easier to get on with his job now that the diary was over, and he wouldn't have to think about things. He'd wrap the diary up and then chuck it away along with the other clearance stuff—as if it had never been found.

Then, when he picked it up to hide it in his shirt, he had one last flip through the pages. One last lingering moment of silence with Pelly D.

Two of the pages were stuck together.

"Come on, Toni V! Your gang's leaving in five!" Monsumi Q leaned against the doorpost. Again, there was no time to hide the diary. He'd definitely have to destroy it now. As soon as he'd read to the end . . .

"Tell 'em to wait up. I'll be right down!"

Mon Q nodded. "Sure thing." And he did.

Fingers clumsy with excitement, Toni V carefully eased the two pages apart. A slip of paper fell out. There was more writing. It was in a different hand. Small and spiky—unlike Pelly D's confident flow.

53rd 1st 153

A nice symmetry in the date there. Only a year since this diary started & only a minute before it's over. Not long to write. Retrievd this fm the recycling bin. I kw why Pelly threw it out. She thks this part of her life is dn & she dt want to be remindd of it. Bt there needs to be a memory.

Wish I hd a diary—smthg to be left of my life when we're gn. All I am now is a few lines in this notebk (can't believe Pelly wrote about me, god I love tt girl) & a memory—a vanishd footfall on the Plaza & an unseen face lkg at the stars. I'm gg out to the Plaza to bury this. Risky. Dt want to be spottd by Security. 15 sqrs in fm the south side, startng at the big name plaque, then 7 sqrs east. There's a flowerbed with a set of saplings that the sawri birds like to peck. I've often watchd thm there. Now they'll hv to peck w-out me. Me n Pelly'll cm bk & dig the diary up & hv a laugh & cry about how thgs w in the War. (She calls it The Rudeness!) No news frm Pelly's dad, to get us out of this mess. He's prob bn encouraged to shed unsuitable relationships. He n I'll hv words when I get bck.

& if someone finds this bef we get bck fm wherevr we're gg, well other people'll read t diary and be glad tht there's Peace & all this mess is over & people can start their lives again. The financial details encl are for an acc in the name of Pelly Damson, a canny stash that only she knew about, bt it shd be safe still—it's authorizd by Pelly's dad. If we ct cm bck & spnd Pelly's credit, someone'll be able to. Find sometg gd for the money. It didn't help her much. I wish she hdn't had to go thru with all ths. Glad I'll be with her whatever.

* * *

Finally—IMPORTANT—people are leaving stuff in all t hiding places they can find. Photos—diaries, evn jt thr names. It matters. Sm people've alrdy buried stuff in the Plaza—people who left earlier ths month. When we cm bk we'll have to dig & find everythng, else no one'll knw we were here.

Pen's running out.

It's hard to quit writing—as if a vital link will be broken when the words stop

"Are you in a bad mood or what?" said Wim Vellora, seeing the scowl on Toni V's face.

"I'm fine," he said.

"Life getting you down, sunshine? I got a nice trip lined up for you—put that smile back on your face."

Toni V straightened up.

"You and Appel F and a coupla others are to go to the docks and help with taking the latest load to landfill, down the east canal. They got a coupla workers short—some lung bug or something. You know where the docks are?"

Toni V nodded, feeling gray inside. It was all very well to know that he was doing the right thing, going back to work. The trouble was, there was no going back to normal.

It was a beautiful day for being on the water—clear blue sky, fresh summer breeze and clouds of scarlet sawri birds wheeling overhead. Toni V hadn't been on a boat since they first got dropped off at City Five. The barge would be better than the sailboat, it wouldn't send his stomach sickening so much. It was already loaded with mini-Dumpsters by the time he and Appel F got there. They jumped aboard and found a spot on the railings up front.

The city slipped away slowly. The tall buildings dwindled and the countryside spread out before them. It was lovely. He could see why the Colonials had picked this place—fields stretching away, groves of trees, the lazy blue water of the canal.

A few miles out of the city the air grew heavy. The water seemed more sluggish. A strange stillness settled on the crew of the boat as it made its way past long low fields on either side of the canal. Here there were no trees, only vivid green grass—new growth—and mad splashes of red and blue flowers. The sawri birds would not even fly near the place. Near the water's edge, the ground was scorched. Toni V turned his face toward the sun and let his eyes be blinded for the moment. Fortunately the landfill wasn't far off.

He jumped ashore and tied the heavy mooring rope to a post on the quay side. While the rest of the crew woke up to the fact that they had to shift and get working, Toni V went for a wander along the bank. He had a lot on his mind. He was half thinking that he could go a little way from the water's edge and maybe just throw the diary into the heavy banks of red flowers that seemed to be thriving on the gray soil. Only a few steps took him away from the *slap-slap* noise of the canal water and into thick stillness. The ground seemed very powdery under his feet. Gray and powdery. Farther away from the shore, he thought he could see strange shapes strangled in the grass. Then his stomach churned: he saw bags and cases, all spilling their emptiness out into the hot air. Something winked in the sun. He bent down.

He had found a square sliver of metal with a fancy raised design and a delicate metal chain. He knew what it was. He'd seen them around the necks of those gorgeous girls by the pool at the end of the water flume. It was a season pass for Waterworld.

With a sudden flash of emotion, he hurled the metal badge away and he did not then go to find it, to see whose name had been written underneath.

The General's slogans sounded manically in his brain: *Back to Work! Back to Normal!*

Back to work it was, then. They had to get the minicontainers off the barge, then haul them a short distance to the giant hole that mechanical diggers had gouged into the earth. It was backbreaking work, but the only way to keep the city free of pollution. They all hauled in silence for a couple of hours.

Toni V's shoulders were red and sore from the tuff-fabric straps used for hauling. He straightened up for a moment at the edge of the landfill. The hole was more than half-full of jagged masonry, blown-up bits of furniture, junk—rubble—everything. On top of it all was a dead cat, with black rotted eyes, shrunken skin, and ribs sticking out. The sun beat down.

Inside his shirt, the diary of Pelly D crackled and made him sweat even more. He got right to the edge of the pit where a scrawny kid in orange overalls was just sending a Dumpster–full over the edge.

This was awkward. Toni V didn't like the idea of gorgeous, giddy Pelly D lying on a pile of junk next to a corpse. He didn't want anyone else to see her like that—think she was just rubbish, something to clear out to make way for The New.

The kid in orange wiped her forehead, leaving a dirty streak in the sweat. "Sure is hot," she said.

"Like an oven," Toni V agreed.

"Not long till water break—small mercies."

"Yeah—not long."

The kid turned to go back with her empty mini-container.

"Hey!" he called out, then clammed up for a moment, not sure what he wanted to say.

"Yep?"

He scratched the silver-and-red stamp on the back of his hand. The diary burned a hot square onto his belly. "You, ah, you know the, ah, Galrezi?" The word sounded funny out loud—foreign, just like when he'd first read it in the diary. People didn't use it much anymore.

The kid just looked at him.

Toni V said, "You know—Galrezi . . . with green stamps on their hands."

The kid shrugged. "Yeah? What about them?"

"I just wondered if you'd seen any around?"

"Why would I want to do that?"

"Where'd they all go then?" Toni V heard his voice crack a little. He hated and dreaded his own curiosity.

The girl squinted at Toni V, waiting for him to

make sense. When he didn't, she shrugged and said, "Dunno. They went somewhere, that's all."

"Oh. Sure. Thanks. That was it. I just thought—something about the war, y'know."

"Oh, that." The kid stared at him with eyes too big for her head. She looked way too small to be hauling Dumpsters. "Thank god that's over," she said. "Only this stuff left now."

The girl set off back to the barge leaving him alone. As she hauled her container away it set off an avalanche of rubbish down into the landfill—a discordant clattering noise in that grave of other people's lives.

When the dust settled, Toni V hovered on the edge of the pit for a moment and rubbed his eyes. He had to tell someone about this; someone had to know. Maybe Monsumi Q . . . he wasn't a bad sort. That would be a start. He had to find people to make them believe the unbelievable. *They went somewhere*, the girl had said. Somewhere they wouldn't be coming back from. Somewhere they wouldn't need bags and cases. Somewhere that didn't accept VIP passes to the best H_2O entertainment in town. And they hadn't just gone—they'd been taken there.

Over in the city plaza a mechanical digger scooped up the remains of the once-proud statues. General Saint-Antel's face—long since vandalized by the victors—was pulverized on the spot. Working in teams of twenty-a-side, strong men hauled the new plaza sign into place. Soon it would be wired up and illuminated in red neon for all the city to see: PLAZA INSIDIAN.

In the last heat of summer the cimarron trees dropped their yellow petals and turned their branches up to the sky.

Toni V turned and stumbled away from the pit. The diary still crackled next to his skin and the words kept Pelly D alive for just that little bit longer.